D G
J
Hc

D1547378

Love Strikes a Devil

Barbara Cartland

Love Strikes a Devil

Thorndike Press • Chivers Press
Waterville, Maine USA   Bath, England

This Large Print edition is published by Thorndike Press, USA and by Chivers Press, England.

Published in 2002 in the U.S. by arrangement with International Book Marketing, Limited.

Published in 2002 in the U.K. by arrangement with Cartland Promotions.

U.S. Hardcover   0-7862-4807-6 (Romance Series)
U.K. Hardcover   0-7540-8825-1 (Chivers Large Print)
U.K. Softcover   0-7540-8826-X (Camden Large Print)

The text of this Large Print edition is unabridged.
Other aspects of the book may vary from the original edition.

Set in 16 pt. Plantin by Al Chase.

Printed in the United States on permanent paper.

British Library Cataloguing-in-Publication Data available

Library of Congress Cataloging-in-Publication Data

Cartland, Barbara, 1902–
    Love strikes a devil / Barbara Cartland.
        p. cm.
    ISBN 0-7862-4807-6 (lg. print : hc : alk. paper)
    1. Satanism — Fiction.   2. Inheritance and succession —
Fiction.   3. England — Fiction.   I. Title.
PR6005.A765 L6567 2002
    823´.912—dc21   2002031980

Love Strikes a Devil

Author's Note

In the second half of the nineteenth century in France there was a boom in the publishing of books on Magic.

Church authorities were worried by a vogue for the Supernatural at a time when anticlericalism was widespread in France.

One consequence of this craze for the occult was that Paris acquired a sinister reputation as a centre for Black Magic.

Many literary young men were talking of Magic, but after a while something even more horrifying came into being, which was Satanism.

One of the best known literary personalities was Marquis Stanislas de Guaita, the poet, who became obsessed with Magic after reading the books by Eliphas Levi, and founded the Kabbalistic Order of the Rose Cross.

Guaita eventually undermined his health and his reason with prolonged nightly vigils as he surrounded himself with old spell books, magic manuscripts, and occult apparatus.

Both he and a poet called Dubus took drugs.

Dubus, as I describe in this book, had hallucinations and died half-mad in a Paris urinal after injecting himself with an overdose of Morphine.

Catholic hostility to Satanism became joined with their dislike of Freemasonry. In an encyclical by Pope Pius IX in 1873 it was stated that Freemasons were throughout the world working on Satan's behalf.

There is no doubt that the Belle Époque, as the period was called, was deeply affected and smeared by the rise of Black Magic.

When the controversy over Dreyfus exploded in 1898, there were widespread fears that sinister attempts were being made in secret to destroy the social order of the nation and even its civilisation.

chapter one

1893

Vincent Mawde thought with a sigh of relief that he had at last found a place where he could stop for the night.

He dismounted and put his horse under a tree.

The animal was too tired to have gone any farther.

Nevertheless, he hobbled his legs so that he should not escape before morning.

Then he looked for a sandy place where he could sleep without, as he had endured last night, feeling a number of stones under his blanket.

He had a tent, if that was the right word for it.

It covered him while he slept and protected him from being bitten by the mosquitoes and other insects to be found in that part of India.

He was tired, very tired.

Yet he looked forward to eating first the meagre fare he had brought with him and having a drink.

This he did.

Then, taking the two bottles of Indian

beer that were left, he walked to the other side of the trees.

He set them down in a small stream which would keep them cool until morning.

When he returned, the sun was sinking down towards the horizon.

It would not be long before it was dark.

But there would be the moon and stars to alleviate the darkness.

He erected his tent and put inside it a thick blanket on which he would sleep.

He certainly would need nothing over him.

He had already pulled off most of the light clothes he was wearing which were those of a low-caste Indian traveller.

He was in disguise, and it was seldom when he travelled that he was himself.

At least now he was on his way back to civilisation.

By the Mercy of God, having completed the mission on which he had been sent, he was still alive.

He was just about to crawl into his tent when he heard the sound of a horse's hoofs approaching him.

He was instantly alert, afraid it might be yet another enemy.

He had already escaped from quite a number.

Then, as the man drew nearer, he could

see the uniform coat he was wearil

Vincent gave a shout of delight!

Holding up his hand in welcome, l
waiting until the young Officer reach
and dismounted.

"Vincent! Is it really you?" the newcomer
asked. "I had almost given up hope of
finding you!"

"I certainly had no idea of seeing you
here, Nicolas!" Vincent Mawde replied.
"But why were you searching for me?"

"I have a lot to tell you," Nicolas Giles
said. "Where can I put my horse?"

"Where I have put mine," Vincent replied, "under the trees."

Without saying any more, Nicolas Giles
led his horse towards the trees.

Vincent Mawde looked after him with a
puzzled expression on his face.

What possible reason could there be for
his fellow-Officer to have come in search of
him in what he thought of as the "back of
beyond"?

In less than a week he would have been
back in Barracks.

It seemed extraordinary.

However, after being alone for so long, it
was good to see a friendly face.

Fewer than five minutes passed before
Nicolas came striding back from the trees.

11

he was pulling off his uniform-coat as he did so.

Vincent had pitched his tent below some rocks, the ruin of which had once been a Temple.

They afforded him both protection from the Sun and somewhere to rest his back.

He was sitting now with his feet stuck out in front of him.

His face, like his body, was darkened.

It would have been difficult even for his nearest relatives to recognise him as a fair-skinned Englishman.

Nicolas joined him, and throwing his coat down on the ground, said:

"I cannot tell you how glad I am to have found you! All I can say about this country is that it is too big, and too hot!"

Vincent laughed.

"I agree with you. At the same time, I would not be anywhere else."

"I am afraid that is where you will have to be!" Nicolas replied.

Vincent looked at him in surprise.

"What do you mean?"

"I was told by the Viceroy to come and find you."

"The Viceroy?" Vincent repeated. "What the hell does he want now?"

Nicolas held out a newspaper.

12

"First of all, Vincent, he sent you this."

Vincent took the newspaper from him and saw that it was open at the "Court Circular."

"It is bad news, I am afraid," Nicolas added.

Vincent glanced down the page and saw that one entry had been underlined.

He read:

DEATH OF THE 4TH MARQUIS OF MAWDELYN
We deeply regret to report the sudden death of the Marquis of Mawdelyn, Lord Lieutenant of Berkshire.

The Marquis had been in ill health for only a few weeks before he died last Thursday.

The head of one of the oldest and most respected families in England, he will be deeply missed both in this country and in his traditional position at court. . . .

There followed a long description of the many positions the late Marquis had held with distinction and the large number of decorations he had been awarded.

The last paragraph read:

The Marquis never married, and his heir is

Captain Vincent Mawde, who is at present serving abroad with his Regiment. Captain Mawde is the son of the late Lord Richard of Mawde, a younger brother of the Marquis.

The Funeral will take place on Saturday at Mawdelyn Priory.

Vincent read the entry to the end.

Then he put down the newspaper and Nicolas said:

"I am sorry, Vincent, and it means, of course, that we shall lose you."

"I suppose I shall have to go home," Vincent agreed.

"That is what the Viceroy said," Nicolas replied, "and he also thought you should do so at once without returning to Barracks."

Vincent raised his eye-brows.

"Why did he say that?"

There was a short pause before Nicolas replied:

"That is another thing I have to tell you. You have an enemy!"

"I am aware of that!" Vincent answered.

"I do not mean the enemies you have just been coping with. There is nothing unusual about them!"

"Then what do you mean?" Vincent asked in bewilderment.

"When you left," Nicolas said, "and you

14

will remember it was in the middle of the night, Jeffrey Wood got to hear of it at once through his Batman."

Vincent knew Jeffrey Wood well.

He was a brother Officer for whom he had no particular liking.

Major Wood resented that he received special treatment because of his involvement in what was secretly referred to as "The Great Game."

Vincent would disappear from Regimental duties for long stretches at a time.

No one asked questions as to where he was.

There was, of course, no particular date known on which he was likely to re-appear.

He was sent on special missions by the Viceroy and the High Command of the Army.

Most of his brother Officers accepted this as a matter of course.

However, Major Jeffrey Wood was jealous that Vincent should be in personal touch with the "Powers That Be."

His sarcastic remarks about favouritism irritated Vincent, although most of the time he paid no attention to what he thought was a childish attitude on the part of a man who was older than he was.

Now he asked:

"What has the 'Galloping Major' been up to?"

"When you left in the middle of the night," Nicolas said, "nobody but me saw you go."

"I remember that." Vincent nodded. "And it was all 'hush-hush' as usual."

"Well, Jeffrey became aware that your room was empty," Nicolas continued, "and before it was daylight he had moved in, just in case somebody else staked a claim on it!"

Vincent laughed.

"That sounds very like the Major's tactics, and I hope he was comfortable!"

"He was murdered!" Nicolas said quietly. "Sometime between the moment he got into your bed and when his Batman called him."

"Murdered?" Vincent exclaimed. "I do not believe it!"

"It is true," Nicolas answered. "The man who did it was caught."

"Who was he?"

"An Indian of no particular importance, and when they persuaded him — somewhat roughly — into telling the truth he said that he had received his orders from England!"

Vincent stared at his friend.

"I do not believe you!" he said. "Who in England could possibly want me killed?"

"Apparently they paid him well, for he

16

had quite a lot of money on him," Nicolas replied.

"It *must* have been the usual Russian stirring up trouble amongst the tribesmen."

"The Viceroy and apparently also the Commander-in-Chief think differently," Nicolas said, "and they have advised you to go home since you are now the Marquis of Mawdelyn, but also to go secretly, and on no account to return to Barracks."

"But you have the man who killed Jeffrey in custody!"

"The Viceroy thinks he is not the only one who has been given instructions to get rid of you. You remember that incident in the Bazaar two months ago?"

Vincent frowned.

Of course he remembered it.

He had been walking back through the Bazaar after a secret meeting with a man who had given him some very valuable information.

Because there had been no reason to visit the man in disguise, he was wearing uniform.

He had appeared to be shopping, as many soldiers did when they were off duty.

The conference, however, had taken longer than he had anticipated.

It was now getting dark and the shops

were lighting up their wares with small oil-lamps or candles.

There were the dark shadows that in India could always be sinister and were best avoided.

Vincent was pushing his way through a crowd of men and women, goats, dogs, donkeys, and the occasional sacred cow.

There were quite a number of soldiers in the vicinity.

One officer whose name he did not know moved up to him in the crowd to say:

"You are Mawde, aren't you? I wanted to ask you . . ."

As he spoke, Vincent saw a stall-holder beckon to him.

He thought he was telling him that he had ready the present he had ordered for one of his friends in England.

"Just a moment," he said to the young Officer, beside him. "I want to speak to that fellow."

He pushed his way through a crowd of children to the stall-holder.

He learnt that his guess was right and the present had just arrived.

The man said he would send it to the Barracks the following morning.

"Thank you, Ali," Vincent said to him. "I am very grateful to you. I will have the money ready when the parcel reaches me."

He turned round to return to where the young Officer was waiting for him.

He saw to his surprise that while he had been away a crowd had gathered.

The Officer was lying on the ground.

He had been stabbed from behind with a long, thin stiletto-like knife and was dead before they could get him to a Doctor.

There was absolutely no reason which anyone could ascertain why a young man who had only recently come out from England should have been murdered.

At the time his Commanding Officer had said to Vincent when they were alone:

"I have a suspicion, Mawde, that, as he was stabbed in the back and you were both in uniform, that knife was meant for you!"

Vincent at the time had thought it was likely.

After so many secret missions there were naturally some people who were suspicious.

They did not say so, but they suspected he was not the ordinary British Officer he pretended to be.

However, as nothing further happened, Vincent had put the incident out of his mind until now.

"There is no doubt at all," Nicolas was saying, "that Jeffrey Wood died because he was in your bed. That is why, Vincent, you must get out of India as quickly as possible."

"I cannot understand it, Nicolas," Vincent remarked. "I can assure you I have never imagined having an enemy in England who dislikes me enough to commit murder!"

"Two!" Nicolas said quietly.

"The whole thing is absurd!" Vincent exclaimed. "But of course I shall do what I am told. I suppose somebody will be kind enough to pack up my belongings and send them home to me?"

"I am sure that will be seen to," Nicolas replied.

"It all sounds very strange," Vincent said. "We expected to be in danger out here, but it is a very different thing when it happens at home!"

"I agree with you," Nicolas said, "and I expect there is an explanation, if we only knew the truth. But apparently the madman, who will of course be hanged, is quite convincing."

"Perhaps he thought it was one way of saving his skin," Vincent suggested.

As he spoke, he saw Nicolas put down the bottle of beer from which he had been drinking, and it was empty.

"Are you still thirsty?" he asked. "Would you like another?"

"Need you ask!" Nicolas replied. "I have been riding all day in this gruelling heat. I would drink the Atlantic if it were available."

"I have two more beers," Vincent said. "I will give you one, and share the second with you."

"It is something I would rather have at the moment," his friend laughed, "than all the Rajah's jewels!"

"I will go and get them," Vincent said, "and it will cheer you up to know I have another blanket. I will toss you to decide who has the tent. It is too small for two."

He got up as he spoke and started to walk back towards the trees.

He was just going to the stream to find the beer when he saw that Nicolas had not taken the bridle off his horse.

Nor had he hobbled the animal as considerately as he had done his horse.

Vincent was extremely fond of animals and always wanted them to be as comfortable as he was himself.

He therefore removed the bridle and made the hobble looser.

Then he gave the tired horse a drink from a collapsible bowl which he had used for his own horse.

This meant going to the stream and back again.

When he had finally unpacked a blanket and picked up the two bottles of beer, he had been away for quite a long time.

Now the sun had completely vanished and, as is usual in the East, there was no twilight.

The stars were already filling the sky.

A full moon was rising behind the mountains, which were just a short distance away to the North.

There were many shadows, but where the moonlight shone it was as easy for Vincent to see his way back as if it had been daylight.

Carrying the two bottles, he walked towards the tent.

As he reached it, he realised that Nicolas must have gone inside.

His feet, from which he had removed his riding-boots, were outside the opening.

"I have brought your beer, Nicolas," he said, "and if you are keeping away from the flies, they have vanished now until morning."

There was no answer.

"Come out!" he said. "I have your blanket for you, and I will toss you for the tent, as I said I would."

He bent down to look inside.

Nicolas continued to lie still and silent.

Vincent pulled up the flap of the tent so that the moonlight illuminated the young man's body.

He was lying on his back, and the moonlight also glimmered on something shining just above his heart.

Before Vincent even touched him he realised that Nicolas was dead.

Charisa came running down the stairs as she heard a carriage draw up outside the front-door.

She had been waiting for over an hour for her father to return.

Now, as he stepped out from an open carriage drawn by two of his brilliant horses, she gave a cry of delight.

"You are back, Papa! I was wondering why you were away so long."

Colonel Lionel Templeton kissed his daughter, and they walked up the steps with his arm round her waist.

"It took longer than I expected," he said, "for the simple reason that the new Marquis has not been to the Priory for so many years."

"So of course you had to tell him all he wanted to know," Charisa said.

"I did my best," the Colonel answered,

"and I only hope he will prove as good a Landlord as his uncle was."

Charisa knew by the note in her father's voice that he was doubtful.

"I hope," she said, "he will at least be generous to the pensioners and of course keep the Alms-Houses going."

"I suppose he will do that," the Colonel agreed, "but he did not seem particularly interested. What he wanted to know was what rents he would receive from the tenants, and if the Farmers were making sure of a good harvest."

They had reached the Study by this time.

As the Colonel walked across to the grog-tray to pour himself out a drink, his daughter sat down on the sofa.

She knew from the way her father had been speaking that something was worrying him.

When he came towards her with a glass in his hand, she asked:

"What is wrong, Papa?"

"Nothing is exactly — wrong," the Colonel replied, "and I suppose it is what I have always wished to happen — although not quite so quickly."

Charisa looked puzzled.

"What is it?" she asked.

"The Marquis has suggested, in a somewhat roundabout manner, I admit, that you should marry him."

Charisa stared at her father in sheer astonishment.

"He suggested that to-day . . . when he has only just arrived?"

"As I said, it was in a roundabout fashion," the Colonel said, "but I did think, my dearest, that he was rather 'rushing his fences.' After all, you cannot have seen him for at least ten years!"

"Fourteen!" Charisa said. "I was working it out this morning. I was four at the time, and there was a party at Christmas to which all the Mawde family had been invited."

"You could hardly have expected him to be your prospective Bridegroom at that age!" the Colonel said.

He put down his glass and walked across the room and back again before he said:

"I will not pretend to you, my dearest, that it has not been at the back of my mind that you might marry the heir of the late Marquis, because we were such good friends."

"I have often thought that was what you were hoping, Papa!" Charisa said. "After all, Mawdelyn Priory means so much to you, and not only because His Lordship relied on you to see to everything for him. I always thought of you as his unpaid Manager!"

"Certainly unpaid," the Colonel agreed, "considering I was obliged to help him in financial matters simply because he never had enough income."

"Do you honestly think," Charisa asked, "that because he was so fond of you, and because you loved him, he did not feel embarrassed by your generosity?"

"Of course not," the Colonel replied. "At the same time, I do not want a young man I have only just met to take it for granted that he can call on my purse whenever it pleases him. Now, in order to make quite certain it will always be available, he is prepared to make you his wife!"

"Do you really mean that is what he is planning?" Charisa asked.

"I have put it rather bluntly," her father said, "but you know, my darling, I am a pretty good judge of men. It was always said in the Regiment that I had an uncanny knack of seeing into a man's soul."

"Of course you have!" Charisa said. "So let us tell the new Marquis that he can find his own friends to pay up for him, and not rely on you."

"I would do that," the Colonel said, "if it was not for Mawdelyn. You were right, dearest child, when you said I love it."

He laughed before he added:

"I often think the Priory means more to me than to the Mawdes themselves. But then, of course your mother was a Mawde, and I can never forget how much it meant to her."

The Colonel had married a cousin of the Marquis — a distant one, but nevertheless she had been a Mawde.

When his father had bought an estate which marched with Mawdelyn Priory, he had no idea how closely the families would be knit.

Lionel Templeton as a young man was very handsome, and very dashing.

He had seen Elizabeth Mawde at one of the first parties to which he had been invited at the Priory.

He had fallen head-over-heels in love with her.

She had also loved him.

It seemed to the family very suitable that their nearest neighbour should have such a close connection with them.

They were also delighted that Elizabeth had married a very rich man.

The Colonel's father had made his fortune in shipping in the North of England.

He had then come South because he

wanted to "live a life of a gentleman."

He came, in fact, from a long line of Country Squires, but had entered the ship-building business when he was a young man.

When he was rich enough to leave it, he wanted to get away from the North.

He wanted to start a new life for himself.

He found exactly the house he liked in Berkshire.

It did not, of course, in any way resemble the Priory, having been built in about the middle of the eighteenth century.

It was, however, in its own way, extremely impressive.

He soon had the estate running so smoothly that it was an example to all his neighbouring Landlords.

It was, therefore, not surprising that when the 4th Marquis of Mawdelyn inherited he should turn to a man of the same age as himself for advice.

Their friendship was satisfactory to both of them.

Charisa had loved "Uncle George," as she had called the late Marquis.

Because her father was so often at the Priory, it became as much a home to her as their own.

There was not a nook or cranny with

which she was not familiar.

She loved the beauty of the ancient rooms.

She delighted in finding her way through the secret passages which had been first built by the monks.

They had been forced to hide as the Catholics were persecuted under Queen Elizabeth.

Later the passages were extended and used by the Royalists to hide from the Cromwellian troops.

If her father had dreamed of her one day living at the Priory, she had somehow felt in her own mind that it was inevitable.

As she grew older, there were, however, very few of the younger generation for her to meet.

Vincent, the Marquis's nephew and heir apparent, had joined a Regiment as soon as he left Oxford and had been posted abroad.

Although he wrote to her and sent her postcards from India, it was not the same as seeing him.

He had been, she thought now, the nicest of the Mawde men.

But she had been very much a little girl in the eyes of the teenaged boy who was eight years older than herself.

Other Mawdes had come and gone, and

the present Marquis, Gervais Mawde, she could hardly remember.

It was a shock when they learnt that Vincent was dead.

"How is it possible that Fate could be so cruel?" she asked her father.

The news had come from India soon after the late Marquis's Funeral.

Her father had been notified by a letter from Gervais Mawde.

He had written to say he was unable to attend the Funeral because he would be in Paris.

But he had learnt of his cousin's death and, since he was next in line, he would be returning to England as soon as possible.

There was, however, a snag.

The Colonel of Vincent's Regiment had reported to the War Office that what was assumed to be his body had been found in some obscure part of the country.

It was, however, not possible to be completely sure that the identification was correct.

Colonel Templeton had gone to London to visit the War Office.

He learnt that while a body had been discovered in Vincent's tent stabbed through the chest, it had been over a week before the English were aware of it.

Owing to decomposition in the extreme heat, it had been difficult to identify it with certainty.

The Colonel had also learned that a brother Officer was missing.

They were still looking for him.

He might be able to give the authorities more information.

However, a month later, under pressure from Gervais Mawde, the War Office was forced to confirm that Vincent was dead.

It was then that Gervais became the 6th Marquis.

Until everything was settled, he had not come to the Priory.

Now he had done so, and the Colonel had met him at his request.

"What is he like?" Charisa asked.

Her father hesitated.

"I had not seen him for many years," he replied, "in fact, it must be, as you say, all of fourteen years ago."

"Does he look like a Mawde?" Charisa enquired.

"Yes, he does," the Colonel admitted, "although there is something about him which makes him different. I expect it is because he has lived abroad for so long, and is more cosmopolitan than the rest of the family."

"Why did he live in France?" Charisa

asked. "I have often wondered why, but no one seemed to have an answer."

"I am told he enjoys Paris, and his mother was half-French. He was also educated there, so all his friends are French."

"It is difficult to think of the Mawdes as being anything but English Country gentlemen," Charisa remarked.

"That is what I think too," the Colonel agreed.

He was silent for a moment before he said:

"I suppose as marriages among French aristocrats are usually arranged, we can understand what Gervais expects of his own marriage. That is why he approached me first instead of getting to know you."

"I think we should make it clear, Papa, that we are English. You have always promised me that I would not be forced to marry anyone I did not love."

"Of course not," the Colonel agreed. "At the same time, my darling, I would like you to meet Gervais with an open mind."

He paused before he went on:

"We must bear in mind the fact that a young man who has been brought up amongst the French will not think or behave in exactly the same way as someone who has gone to Eton, Oxford, and then inevitably into the family Regiment."

"I do understand that," Charisa said. "But, Papa, I have no wish to be married in a hurry to anyone! I love being with you, and I love my home."

"You also love Mawdelyn," her father said quietly.

"It is beautiful, I grant you," Charisa replied, "but it is only made of bricks and stone."

She paused for a moment before she went on:

"You loved Mama and Mama loved you. What I want is to be married to a man with whom I am happy, not because he possesses anything in particular, but just because he is he."

The Colonel looked at his daughter.

Then he put his arms round her and kissed her.

"That is what I want for you, my dear," he said fondly. "But we are dining at the Priory to-night, and, as I have already said, we must both meet Gervais with an open mind."

chapter two

Driving with her father towards the Priory, Charisa was thinking of Vincent.

She had wished so many times since she had heard of his death that he could have become the new Marquis.

Then everything would have gone on as it had in the past.

She as a small girl had adored Vincent, although he had ordered her about.

He made her bowl to him when he was practising Cricket, and "fag" for him in every way when he was home from School.

But he had always been kind and understanding.

She could remember crying on his shoulder when she had been stung by a wasp.

He had carried her home when she had fallen down and hurt her foot.

"Why did he have to die?" she asked angrily.

By the time they reached the Priory she was, although she would not admit it, nervous.

It seemed ridiculous, when going to the

Priory in the past had always been like going home.

She often thought she had spent her life until now more at the Priory than in her father's house.

Certainly all its amenities had been available to her — the horses, the lake on which she could propel a small canoe, the hot-house gardens with their fruit and flowers, and, of course, every room in the house itself.

She played the piano in the Music-Room because the room was larger and the piano was a superior instrument to their own.

She took any book she wanted to read from the Library.

The servants at the Priory had spoilt her ever since she was a tiny child.

"I suppose," she said to her father just before they turned into the drive, "Gervais is delighted to find such a splendid staff waiting for him."

"He did murmur something about bringing in some younger servants," the Colonel replied.

Charisa gave a cry of protest.

"How could he think of doing anything so foolish?" she demanded. "Most of the families have served there generation after generation, and if there is anyone extra required, they should come from the village."

Her father did not answer.

She knew he was thinking that neither of them could interfere with the new Marquis, except perhaps very tactfully.

This was another thing which made Charisa feel nervous.

He might make alterations which she was sure would be wrong for the Priory itself.

They walked in through the great oak door which led into the huge Hall in which the monks had originally eaten their meals.

It was also where they had received visitors.

It had been traditional that anyone who was hungry or in need of spiritual guidance was welcome.

To Charisa, the spirits of the monks still lingered in the Hall.

Every time she came into the house she felt they welcomed her.

There was, however, now only the Butler, old Dawkins, who had been at the Priory for forty years.

"Good-evening, Miss Charisa!" he said in his courtly voice. "Good-evening, Sir."

"Here I am again, Dawkins!" the Colonel said. "I hope everything is all right and to His Lordship's liking."

"We can only hope, Sir, there won't be too many changes," Dawkins replied.

Charisa glanced at her father, but there was nothing either of them could say.

They followed Dawkins towards the Drawing-Room.

This was one of the most beautiful rooms in the Priory and had been redecorated by her mother at the old Marquis's request.

Mrs. Templeton had made it very beautiful.

She had moved into it some Louis XIV furniture which had come to the Priory after the French Revolution.

Hanging on the white panelled walls were pictures of the same period.

Those she had collected from the Picture Gallery and other parts of the house.

The crystal chandeliers were unique and very beautiful.

So were the mirrors which had also been brought to England at the same time from Italy.

The Mawdes had been great travellers and had also held many diplomatic posts abroad.

This meant that the Priory had become a Treasure House for the many priceless gifts which they had received.

Other unique and lovely objects they had

discovered for themselves in different parts of the world.

Charisa as a small girl had loved the pieces of Greek statuary which one Mawde had carried home in triumph.

She had also loved the porcelain guard-dogs from China which warded off evil spirits.

But she could not believe there were any evil spirits in the Priory.

To her the atmosphere always seemed to be charged with a sanctity.

It was what the monks had brought there when they had built it with their own hands.

It had been decorated to the glory of God, and when she was small her mother had told her its story.

She used to imagine the monks praying as they laid brick upon brick, singing as they cut down the trees in order to make beams or the floor-boards.

The recent decorations had screened the primitive efforts of the monks in making everything look as perfect as possible.

Everywhere Charisa looked she saw beauty.

Yet she was sure the monks were still as proud of the Priory as they had been when they first built it.

The chandeliers were all lit in the Drawing-Room, which had not happened for some years.

The late Marquis had not entertained

very much after Vincent went to India.

It made the room seem very festive as they entered it.

Charisa guessed that the new Marquis was making his dinner-party a "gathering of the Clan."

Everybody present was related, and, of course, Charisa and the Colonel knew them well.

There were the two elderly sisters of the late Marquis who lived in the Dower House.

They seldom went out to dinner.

There were quite a number of cousins who had houses within driving distance of the Priory.

Some had been given a house actually on the estate.

There was no one young except for two men of about twenty-five.

Charisa knew they had come a long distance to be present this evening.

She looked round at those who were present before she was acutely aware of the one stranger amongst them.

Gervais, as they were announced, had his back to them.

Then, as Dawkins said their names, he turned round.

At first glance Charisa thought he was very much a Mawde.

He had the same square forehead, the clear-cut features which were characteristic of all the men in the family.

But because he had French ancestry, his hair and his eyes were darker.

As he walked towards them, she realised he was not tall, and there was also something different about him to which she could not quite put a name.

He reached the Colonel first and held out his hand.

"It is delightful to see you again," he said.

Then he looked at Charisa.

"Is this my beautiful cousin about whom I have heard so much?" he enquired.

Charisa smiled at him.

"I think I should say 'Welcome to the Priory'!" she answered. "In fact we have not met since I was four years old!"

"How can I have been so remiss as not to have come to England until now?" the Marquis asked. "I might have guessed that a lovely child would grow into a very beautiful woman!"

It was a pretty speech, but Charisa felt it came too glibly from his lips.

She was sure it was something he must have said many times before.

Then she chided herself for being critical.

After all, she had promised her father she

40

would meet Gervais with an open mind.

She went round the other relations.

She kissed the old aunts from the Dower House affectionately as she said:

"I have never known you to come out to dinner before, and you know how often Papa and I have invited you to do so."

"I know, dearest child," one of the old ladies answered, "but Cousin Gervais was so insistent that we found it impossible to refuse."

It sounded to Charisa as if Gervais was determined to make himself pleasant to everybody.

He paid the ladies compliments which made some of them blush with surprise.

He was very genial to the men.

"You have a lot to teach me because I have been living in France," he said disarmingly. "So you must all tell me what I do wrong, and I promise you I shall be grateful and not in the least resentful."

"We will do our best to turn you into a Country Gentleman," one of the relations said heartily. "I suppose you enjoy riding? There has never been a Mawde who is not completely at home on a horse."

"I ride every day in the Bois when I am in Paris," Gervais answered, "but I know before you tell me so that it is not the same as hunting or riding over rough ground."

They laughed at this, and Charisa thought he was being very clever.

He was making them all feel that he wanted them, just as he had been clever enough to ask her father's advice as soon as he arrived.

He sat at the top of the table in the chair which had always seemed to Charisa like a throne.

It was carved with the Arms of the Mawde family and he looked almost regal.

As usual at the Priory, the food was delicious.

It was served by Dawkins and the footmen in the quiet, efficient manner which had always been to the admiration of any guest who stayed there.

There was champagne to drink as well as some excellent white wine.

Charisa saw her father look at his glass with an expression of surprise.

She guessed it was a wine which the new Marquis must have brought with him from France.

There was certainly a great deal of it.

By the end of dinner any shyness on the part of the Mawde family had vanished.

They were laughing and talking with an enthusiasm which was unusual, especially amongst the older members of the family.

As the meal ended, the Marquis said to the Lady on his right:

"Now you have to instruct me. As you know, in Paris the gentlemen leave the Dining-Room with the ladies. But here I must behave as an Englishman, so will you take the Ladies away? I will then produce some stories which are not suitable for your shell-like ears."

The Lady to whom he was speaking laughed before she rose to her feet, and the other women followed her.

When they reached the Drawing-Room they all began talking at once.

"He is charming, really charming!"

"Of course, some of the things he says are very French, but he will soon become more like us."

"I must say, I was nervous when I came here this evening. Now I am completely bowled over by him!"

They were all saying very much the same thing over and over again.

Charisa went upstairs to the room which she knew would be open and ready for any guest who wished to tidy herself.

The elderly Housekeeper was waiting there and exclaimed as soon as she saw her:

"I was hoping to see you, Miss Charisa."

"Good-evening, Mrs. Bush," Charisa said. "Is everything all right?"

The Housekeeper paused before she replied:

"I hope so, Miss, I hope so with all me heart, but I'm not going to say too much too soon!"

"His Lordship seems very eager to please," Charisa said a little tentatively.

"That's what Mr. Dawkins tells me," Mrs. Bush said, "but I've a feeling in my bones there'll soon be changes!"

"Now, what makes you say that?" Charisa asked.

"It's just something I knows as sure as I'm standing here!" Mrs. Bush replied. "Well, I 'pects if anything goes wrong, the Colonel'll help us."

"Of course he will, and I think you are just frightening yourself unnecessarily," Charisa said.

She saw the expression of worry on the Housekeeper's face, and added:

"If ever you want my father to help you, all you have to do is to send a groom to him with a note. You know he will come at once and try to sort things out."

"I'm hoping, Miss, there will be no need to worry the Colonel," Mrs. Bush replied, "but something tells me that it's no use expecting too much."

Charisa sat down at the dressing-table and tidied her hair.

As she did so, one of her older Mawde cousins came into the room.

It was therefore no longer possible to talk to Mrs. Bush.

At the same time, she was anxious as she went back to the Drawing-Room.

She knew that neither Dawkins nor Mrs. Bush would be looking for trouble.

In fact, she suspected they were afraid the Marquis would consider them too old.

They had neither of them any wish to retire.

'Gervais would not be so stupid as to send them away when the entire household depends on them,' she thought.

Nevertheless, she felt apprehensive.

Perhaps he wanted French servants at the Priory, and that would be a mistake.

It was considered an honour for any girl or boy to be taken into service at the Big House.

They would object strongly to being deprived of the privilege.

Especially, she added to herself, if the intruder was of a different nationality.

The villagers and the estate resented foreigners.

"I am certain Papa has explained that to

the Marquis," she told herself as she re-entered the Drawing-Room.

The ladies were still talking about the Marquis.

"It is surprising," one of them said, "that he is not married! After all, he is over thirty, because Simon, his father, married long before Richard, and therefore Gervais was always the oldest nephew."

"I was so very fond of Vincent," one of the cousins said in a sad voice.

"So was I," another agreed. "I often thought, considering he was the heir presumptive to George, it was a great mistake for him to be in the Army and risk his life."

"What I think is strange," another cousin said, "is that his body has not been sent home to be interred in the family Vault! Surely somebody should have told the Commanding Officer of Vincent's Regiment that was what we would all expect?"

"I think Papa did mention it at the War Office," Charisa chimed in, "but as you know, there was some difficulty in identifying whether the body found was Vincent's or somebody else's."

"Anyway, they must have made up their minds now," an elderly aunt said sharply, "otherwise Gervais would not have been

46

allowed to assume the title."

She paused before she said to Charisa:

"I shall speak to your father and say he must go to the War Office again and insist that Vincent is decently buried with all the other Mawdes!"

Charisa moved away.

It upset her to hear them talking about Vincent.

She had only to look out of the window to feel that she could see him moving in the garden.

He had loved the great hedges with their topiary work.

He had practised Archery on the long green lawn she could now see from where she was standing.

"Why do you want to use a bow and arrow when you can use a gun?" she had asked when she was very small.

"Because I want to be proficient at both!" he had answered. "A bow and arrow is actually more difficult than shooting with a gun. Try it for yourself."

When she first tried she found it difficult, being so small, to pull back the string.

Vincent had helped her.

When she grew older she would challenge him to a contest as to who could score the most points.

Invariably he won, but she liked being with him.

When he went shooting he allowed her to go with him to carry what he shot in a game-bag.

Now the Gentlemen joined the Ladies.

As they did so, Charisa realised one of the reasons Gervais looked different was that his clothes seemed too close-fitting.

Perhaps, for want of a better word, he was too smart.

There was nothing casual or comfortable about him.

Watching him, she thought he was also very much on the alert.

He was ready with his compliments, his jokes, his ingratiating way of asking for assistance.

'He is too polished,' she thought, and again rebuked herself for being critical.

Towards the end of the evening, when some of the older relatives were asking for their carriages, Gervais said to the Colonel:

"I have a suggestion to make to which I hope you will agree."

"What is it?" the Colonel asked.

"As I have so much to discuss with you and, as you know, so much to learn, would you and Charisa come and stay here for a few days? Or should I say for at least a week or so?"

The Colonel looked surprised.

"Do you really want us?"

"More than I can tell you," Gervais replied. "First, because I have no wish to be alone. Secondly, because I have some friends coming from Paris whom I want you to meet, and thirdly, because, quite selfishly, I need your help."

He spoke so sincerely that it was impossible for the Colonel to do anything but say:

"Very well, of course, if I can really be of assistance."

"I cannot begin to tell you how grateful I would be if you would do as I ask," Gervais said, "and I am sure Charisa will show me all the best places to ride better than anybody else could do."

Ever since the Marquis's death, Charisa had been to the Priory two or three times a week to help exercise the horses.

Her father had said:

"You know as well as I do that the grooms will become lax if there is nobody to keep an eye on them! Therefore, my dearest, you should make it quite clear that you will not only ride the horses, but also inspect them."

Charisa knew exactly what he meant.

Abbey, the Head Groom, was getting old and suffered from rheumatism.

Because he was not always about, the

young grooms were inclined to be slack in their duties.

The one thing Charisa could not bear was that the horses might suffer in any way.

They had been acquired for the late Marquis by her father.

She suspected that he had also paid for quite a number of them.

As the Marquis had become older, he had found it a bore to drive a long distance.

And he was not well enough to ride.

However, he still liked to think that his stables were in good condition.

He wanted good horses there when Vincent returned from India.

They could also be ridden by any of his relatives who came to the Priory to see him.

It was therefore the Colonel who had stocked the stables for him.

He insisted on their being in the same perfect condition as his own.

In fact, Charisa often found it difficult to remember which horses belonged to the Marquis and which to her father.

As far as she was concerned, all she wanted to do was to ride them.

She gave them all an equal part of her affection.

Now she smiled at the Marquis as she said:

"Of course I will do that. There are places in the woods you will love, just as there are some flat fields which make excellent gallops."

"Then we will explore them to-morrow," he said, " and I shall be looking forward eagerly to your arrival."

When a little later they said good-night, he repeated what he had said just to make sure they would not change their minds.

Charisa held out her hand.

"Good-night, Cousin Gervais," she said, "and thank you for a delicious dinner!"

Gervais took her hand in his and unexpectedly raised it to his lips.

He actually kissed the softness of her skin.

It was not the perfunctory gesture it normally was.

Then, as he did so, Charisa felt suddenly a very strange sensation move through her.

For a moment she could hardly believe what she felt was true.

Gervais released her hand, and she ran down the steps to where the carriage was waiting.

As she did so she knew what she had felt was a feeling of repugnance.

"But . . . why? Why?" she asked herself, and could find no reasonable explanation for it.

She drove with her father for a long time in silence before the Colonel asked:

"Now that you have seen him — what do you think?"

"I was just going to ask you the same question," Charisa replied.

"He is certainly a very good host," the Colonel conceded, "and he went out of his way to be exceedingly pleasant to everybody."

"You are still not telling me what you really think of him, Papa!" Charisa said.

"To be quite frank, my dearest, I do not know," the Colonel replied. "I suppose I thought him a little too glib, and that he was trying too hard to be disarming."

"Do you think he expected criticism?" Charisa asked.

"Of course he did!" the Colonel replied. "He is obviously intelligent. He is well aware that because he has lived all his life in France, his relatives are suspicious of everything about him."

"I can see that," Charisa agreed, "and you are right, Papa."

"I think, in the circumstances, he has taken his first fences extremely cleverly," the Colonel said.

"After dinner," Charisa said, "everybody in the Drawing-Room was saying how charming they thought him to be."

"That is exactly what he wanted them to do," the Colonel answered, "and he certainly made himself very much at home among the men."

"Then I suppose we should not be critical," Charisa said in a small voice.

She was still thinking, as she spoke, of what she had felt when he had kissed her hand.

'It must have been because he took me by surprise,' she thought. 'Englishmen do not go about kissing the hands of unattached young ladies.'

However, she found it impossible to dismiss it lightly.

It had been like a streak of lightning.

She did not wish to discuss with her father what had happened.

Yet she knew she would continue to think about it.

When she reached home she said goodnight.

She was just going up to her bed-room when she said:

"Do not let us go too early to the Priory to-morrow, Papa. I have a lot of things to do here before we leave."

"I feel the same," her father answered. "We will arrive at tea-time. That will be quite soon enough."

When she reached her bed-room Charisa thought — and it was a strange thing for her to think — why did she not want to go to the Priory?

She had always been so thrilled to be going there in the past.

It was something which happened frequently because the late Marquis would insist upon their staying the night.

She had thought of it then as an adventure, and something she enjoyed more than anything else.

Now, surprisingly, she was reluctant to leave her home.

Even the thought of the horses waiting for her in the stables was no compensation.

She went to the window to look out into the darkness.

"Why do I feel like this?" she asked herself. "Why do I not accept him as our other relatives have done as somebody very pleasant and charming?"

Finally, when she had undressed and got into bed she told herself she was being very stupid.

The Priory was an important part of her life.

The Mawde family to which she belonged through her mother were all very close to her heart.

"I have to . . . like him . . . I have . . . to!" she said aloud.

Even as she spoke she felt something strange within herself shrinking from the thought of him, recoiling in horror at the touch of his lips.

"It is something he must not do again," she told herself.

It was a long time before she could fall asleep.

"The trouble is," Charisa told herself the next morning, "we were rather keyed up last night."

Everything that happened had been exaggerated simply because there was a new Marquis at the Priory.

Looking back into its history, she supposed there had been other times when unknown members of the family had inherited the title.

They too must have felt, like the new Marquis, that they had to make a good impression.

"He was understandably over-acting . . . that is what was wrong," Charisa finally decided.

When she went down to breakfast she found her father reading a letter which had just been delivered.

"Good-morning, my dearest," he greeted her. "To tell the truth, it is inconvenient to have to leave here to-day. There are several people who particularly want to see me. I shall have to tell them to come to the Priory, or else drive backwards and forwards to my own house."

"Just send a message to the Marquis saying you are unavoidably prevented from accepting His Lordship's invitation," Charisa suggested.

Her father smiled.

"That is what I would like to do, but you are well aware it is something we cannot do, considering he is relying on me, and, of course, you."

"I have no wish for him to rely on me," Charisa said sharply.

She helped herself from the silver *entrée* dishes which stood on the sideboard.

Then she seated herself at the table before she continued:

"Now, listen, Papa. If he says one more word to you about marrying me, make it clear that it is something which should not be discussed for months . . . in fact for at least six."

Her father looked at her searchingly before he asked:

"Are you telling me that you have taken

a dislike to Gervais?"

"Not exactly a dislike," Charisa said thoughtfully, "but he is very . . . strange and quite different from Vincent and, for that matter, from Uncle George."

She hesitated, then continued:

"I think it is not unreasonable to ask him for time to see how he 'shapes up,' as you might say."

The Colonel laughed.

"I know exactly what you are thinking, and, of course, you are right! There is no hurry, and when it comes to marriage, as you well know, all I want is your happiness, your *real* happiness with a man who is worthy of you."

Charisa smiled at her father.

"Thank you, Papa. You always understand, and I know, although he is a Mawde, Mama would want me to wait and see before I make a decision one way or the other."

"Of course," the Colonel agreed. "Leave it to me, my dearest. I can only think, as I said before, he is doing things in a French way instead of taking his time, in the English manner, which is much more sensible."

" 'Taking his time' is exactly the right expression," Charisa agreed.

Charisa rode with her father in the morning as he was visiting one of his Farms.

When they returned for luncheon there was a large bouquet of orchids on one of the tables.

Charisa looked at it in surprise.

Then she saw there was also a note for her father.

"The flowers and note were delivered half-an-hour ago, Miss Charisa, by a groom from the Priory," the Butler explained.

"I imagined that was where they must have come from," she replied, "please have them put in water for me."

"Very good, Miss Charisa."

She would have turned away, but the Butler said:

"There's a card with the flowers, Miss."

Charisa saw the card and picked it up.

It said:

To the most beautiful of my cousins. With love from Gervais.

She read it with surprise before handing it to her father.

The Colonel was reading the note he had received.

"Gervais is hoping we have not forgotten

his invitation and is expecting us as soon after luncheon as we can manage," he announced.

He then looked at the card his daughter had handed him.

Just for a moment there was a frown between his eyes.

Then he said quietly so that the servants would not overhear him:

"Very French — and once again he is 'rushing his fences!' "

The way he spoke made Charisa laugh.

As she walked upstairs she told herself it was a mistake to take Gervais too seriously.

He was putting on an act and performing very cleverly.

At the same time, neither she nor her father need be deceived by it.

She reached her bed-room.

As she went in, she was thinking that if her father were not a very rich man, Gervais would not be so attentive!

The same applied to her.

He must have known many women in Paris whom he could have married if he had wished to do so.

But perhaps as he was not then as important as he was now, she reasoned, *they* would not entertain the idea.

'The French are very practical in such

matters,' she thought.

Alternatively, they might not be heiresses as she would be as her father's only child.

"He may be able to 'pull the wool' over most people's eyes," she told herself, "but not mine!"

Having changed her riding-clothes for a very pretty gown, she went downstairs to find her father waiting for her.

"Luncheon is ready," he said, "but there is no hurry. I have no intention of going to the Priory until the time we have already agreed."

"I thought you would say that," Charisa said.

She slipped her arm through her father's as they walked down the corridor towards the Dining-Room.

"I love you, Papa," she said, "and I am so glad you are not going to be 'stampeded' by an untrained horse."

"Hardly untrained," her father replied. "I think it is more a question of being over-trained, or perhaps, to put it another way, over-eager."

Charisa smiled before she said:

"It seems a little unkind, but I cannot help feeling that your money has a great deal to do with it."

Her father nodded.

"I realised that yesterday when Gervais told me that he was extremely hard up."

Charisa looked at her father in consternation.

"Are you saying he has no money at all?"

"Very little," the Colonel replied. "In fact, Matthews warned me when I was talking to him about Vincent's death that Gervais's father was in debt when he died."

Charisa knew that Matthews was the Solicitor to the Mawdelyn Estate.

"Apparently," her father went on, "the Marquis paid up what was owed and gave Gervais an allowance every year as he did to quite a number of the Mawde family."

He did not say anything else for a moment, and Charisa waited.

Then, as she knew her father was debating with himself whether he should say any more, she begged:

"Tell me the rest!"

"Well, according to Matthews," the Colonel said, "Gervais was certainly overdrawn and always asking the Marquis for more. He warned him several times that he was not the only member of the family in need, but as he was a kind man, he usually paid up."

"No wonder Gervais was delighted at coming into the title!" Charisa said. "And having a great deal more money than he has ever had before."

"It is not enough to keep the house and the estate going as it is now," the Colonel remarked.

"Unless you give him the same assistance as you gave his uncle."

"I helped George because I was very fond of him," her father explained, "but it is a rather different thing to be saddled with a young man I have never seen until yesterday and who has a reputation for over-spending."

"Then that is why he thinks his only way to survive is to marry me!" Charisa said.

Unexpectedly, her father brought his hand down sharply on the table.

"I will not have you pressured into doing anything you do not wish to do!"

"Thank you, Papa! In which case, what are you going to do about Gervais?"

"I will help him in a small way until I am quite certain it is the right thing for me to do," her father replied, "but, like you, I will not be pressured!"

They both laughed.

Then Charisa said:

"In a way, it upsets me. I hate to think of all this intrigue going on at the Priory. But, I suppose, like any young man, he is desperate and clutching at straws."

"That is just what he may prove to be,"

her father said. "In the meantime, we both agree, you will think it over and do nothing hastily."

"You are so sensible, Papa," Charisa said. "At the same time, it is going to be difficult. So I suggest we do not stay at the Priory any longer than is necessary."

"We will return home the very moment you ask me to do so," the Colonel said as he smiled, "but I am quite certain Gervais will be too clever, and there will be other people there, so that you may find you are enjoying yourself."

"I . . . hope so . . . Papa," Charisa said.

At the same time, there was a doubtful note in her voice that was inescapable.

chapter three

Charisa was still running around with things she had to tidy or put away when the carriage came to the door.

She knew her father hated to keep the horses waiting.

She therefore pushed a vase and several other small objects into her maid's arms, saying:

"Put these away for me, Mary, and do not hide them so that I cannot find them again when I come back."

Her lady's-maid, who had been with her for some years, laughed.

"I'll do that, Miss, an' come 'ome soon, we misses you when you're not 'ere."

"As I miss you," Charisa replied.

When they went to the Priory she never took her lady's-maid.

The housemaids whom she had known since she was a small child liked to look after her themselves.

Her father took his Valet, as he refused to go anywhere without him.

Wilkins had already gone ahead with the luggage.

He would have everything unpacked and ready for her father as soon as he arrived.

Picking up the shady hat that went with the gown she was wearing, Charisa ran down the stairs.

The Colonel was waiting in the hall.

"Come along! Come along!" he said in what she called his "Regimental Voice." "We are keeping the horses waiting!"

Charisa only smiled.

At the same time, she hurried down the steps and into the open carriage.

As her father climbed in and they started off, she said:

"It really is a nuisance going to the Priory when there are so many things I should be doing at home! But I am sure, whatever he feels about me, Gervais cannot do without you."

"You are right about that," her father said. "I have come to the conclusion he knows very little about the English way of life, and it is not going to be easy for him at his age to learn new tricks."

Charisa laughed.

"I am sure you will find that he is adaptable, and at least he is willing to learn."

"He is certainly very civil about it," the Colonel replied grudgingly.

They drove on down the narrow lanes.

Looking around her, Charisa thought the countryside was beautiful.

She loved it in the Spring, when there were daffodils, primroses, and violets everywhere.

She loved it too now that it was Summertime.

Bees were humming round the honeysuckle and the crops were golden in the fields.

She knew it was entirely due to her father that the crops at Mawdelyn were almost as good as his own.

'Gervais ought to be very, very grateful to Papa,' she thought.

The horses had reached the outskirts of the village.

As they did so, the Vicar ran out from the gate of the Vicarage waving his arms.

Without being told, the Coachman brought the horses to a standstill.

The Vicar, who was a middle-aged man, his hair greying at the temples, came to the side of the carriage.

"I was just coming to call on you, Colonel!" he said.

"I am sorry, Vicar," the Colonel replied, "but Charisa and I have been asked to stay at the Priory, and that is where we are going now."

The Vicar looked so worried that the Colonel added:

"What did you want to see me about? Is it important?"

"I think it is," the Vicar answered. "I hate to delay you, but would it be possible for you to come into the Vicarage for a few minutes?"

"Of course we can," the Colonel replied.

"It is very kind of you," the Vicar said in an apologetic voice, "and I dislike being a nuisance, but I do need your advice."

The Coachman and the footman on the box had, of course, heard what he said.

As the Vicar hurried to open the gate which led into a small driveway, the horses were turned back.

They drove through the gate and up to the house.

It was a very attractive Vicarage which had been built over fifty years ago and was, Charisa knew, very comfortable.

It was also on the large side now that the Vicar's children had all grown up and left home.

She noted how pretty the garden looked, which was Mrs. Taylor's pet hobby.

As they entered the hall, there was the fragrance of roses from an arrangement on one of the tables.

The room into which the Vicar took them had several vases of flowers in it also.

It was, as Charisa knew, his particular sanctum, where he wrote his sermons.

The walls were covered with books, and he had up to a year ago tutored her in English Literature.

He was an extremely intelligent man, and she had loved her lessons with him.

They usually ended in discussions not only on English Literature, but also on every other subject possible.

She had often thought how very lucky she was to have somebody living in the village who could tell her so many things she wanted to know, not only about the present world, but the whole growth of civilisation from its very beginning.

She had, in fact, met the Vicar earlier that morning.

She had gone into the village to buy something from the shop which sold everything anyone in the vicinity could possibly want.

This was the reason he had not greeted her again.

Now, as she settled herself in a comfortable chair, he said:

"You will forgive me, Charisa, if you are in a hurry to reach the Priory."

"I am in no hurry," Charisa replied. "In

fact, if we are truthful, neither Papa nor I really have the time to stay there."

As she spoke, she realised the Vicar was not listening.

He was looking at her father, and it was obvious that he was very worried.

"Well, what is the trouble, Vicar?" the Colonel asked.

"I went to call at the Priory this morning," the Vicar began, "and after waiting for some time, as I understood His Lordship had not yet come down to breakfast, I was at last able to meet him."

The Colonel was listening.

However, Charisa knew her father was wondering what could have happened and why the Vicar seemed to be in such an agitated state.

"As you know," he continued, "I had not met the Marquis before, as I did not come here until twelve years ago."

"That is right, I remember that," the Colonel agreed, "and we have all thought since then how lucky we have been to have you."

"As you know," the Vicar went on, "the late Marquis was very kind to me, and extended to me his friendship. I have, in fact, been very happy here."

"As I hope you will continue to be for

many more years to come!" the Colonel responded.

"It is about that that I wish to consult you," the Vicar replied.

The Colonel looked surprised.

Charisa was aware that he had sat up a little stiffly in his chair.

"What happened this morning?" he asked sharply.

"I welcomed His Lordship, then told him I was the present Incumbent of the parish and I expressed the hope that I would be able to serve him as I had his uncle before him."

There was silence, then, as no one spoke, the Vicar said:

"His Lordship did not seem to know that the Living was in his gift. When I explained to him that whoever became the Marquis of Mawdelyn had the right to appoint the Incumbent of the parish and also to pay him, he seemed surprised.

" 'I am not only Minister to the village and the estate, My Lord,' I said, 'I am also Your Lordship's Private Chaplain.'

"He stared at me, but he did not speak, and I continued:

" 'Your Lordship's uncle attended the Services in the Parish Church and always read a lesson.'

" 'Read a lesson?' His Lordship exclaimed.

" 'Yes, My Lord,' I replied. 'It is a tradition which goes back several generations.' "

"Yes, of course!" the Colonel interposed. "I should have thought he might have been aware of that!"

"I then explained to His Lordship," the Vicar continued, "that once a month I hold the Service in the large Chapel at the Priory because it is not always easy for the whole household, especially when there is a party, to come to the Services in the Parish Church."

"I have always thought that a very sensible arrangement," Charisa said. "Some of the house-maids are far too old to have to hurry to Church and hurry back when there is so much to do both in the morning and in the evening."

"I was just about to explain that to His Lordship," the Vicar said, "when he told me he was bringing his own Private Chaplain over from France!"

For a moment both the Colonel and Charisa were silent in astonishment.

Then the Colonel exclaimed:

"His own Private Chaplain? Good gracious — do you imagine that having lived in France the Marquis is a Roman Catholic?

The idea never occurred to me!"

"He did not say so," the Vicar said. "He merely said that my services would no longer be required at the Priory!"

He looked more worried than ever as he went on:

"I also had the feeling, Colonel, that he might put his Private Chaplain in my position!"

"No, of course he could not do that!" the Colonel said. "You are indispensable to the whole village, and everybody in the neighbourhood is very fond of you."

"That is true," Charisa interjected. "I think there would be a revolution if Gervais even suggested your leaving here!"

"I must emphasise," the Vicar said quickly, "that His Lordship did not say that he wished me to go. I only felt that the idea was in his mind when he was speaking of his Chaplain."

"Did he say whether he was French or English?" the Colonel demanded.

The Vicar shook his head.

The Colonel thought for a moment. Then he said:

"You must leave this to me. I will explain to Gervais how indispensable you are, not only to those on the estate, but also in the village, and in fact your reputation has spread all over the County."

He paused before he continued:

"The Chief Constable, General Sir Mortimer Stanbrook, was saying to me only a few weeks ago that the speech you made at the Yeomanry Dinner was one of the best they have ever listened to!"

"That is very gratifying," the Vicar said, "and you know, Colonel, both my wife and I would be very unhappy if we had to leave here."

The Colonel rose to his feet.

"Leave it to me," he said. "Gervais does not understand English ways, and I will make sure that he does not discontinue the monthly Services in the Chapel. I will also make it very clear to him in no uncertain terms that we need you."

"I knew I could rely on you, Colonel," the Vicar said in a tone of relief.

He put out his hand and the Colonel shook it.

"Now, do not worry," he said. "As we all know, 'New brooms sweep clean.' In fact, I have already found that the new Marquis is much too quick off the mark in more ways than one!"

Charisa thought this was very true.

She rose and kissed the Vicar on the cheek as she said:

"Papa is quite right. We cannot do without you. I know there is not a single person in this part of Berkshire who will not say the same thing."

"Thank you, Charisa," the Vicar replied.

As they drove away, he waved to them from his front-door.

Charisa could see that he looked very much happier than when they had first arrived.

As they passed through the gate and were back on the road to the village, she said to her father:

"Gervais must be mad if he is thinking of sacking the Vicar when he is such a brilliant and outstanding person!"

"I suppose Gervais had no idea of that," the Colonel replied. "It never occurred to me that I should tell him how important the Vicar was in local affairs."

"You must tell him now," Charisa said, "and make him stop his Chaplain from coming to England."

When her father did not speak, Charisa added:

"I never imagined that Gervais would be particularly religious."

"Nor did I," the Colonel agreed. "But do not worry, my dear, I will find out what all this is about and make Gervais see sense."

"I hope we are not in for any more shocks!" Charisa remarked. "I did not tell you, but Mrs. Bush hinted yesterday that there might be changes in the staff."

"Good Heavens!" the Colonel exclaimed. "He is not thinking of getting rid of her, or of Dawkins. If he does that, the roof will cave in!"

"That is what I thought," Charisa said. "Oh, Papa, do talk to him as soon as possible, and make him understand that he will ruin the Priory if he tries to change things. No one wants modern ideas or modern people, when everything is perfect just as it is!"

"I will do my best," the Colonel said. "At the same time, as you well know, the Marquis of Mawdelyn can be a 'law unto himself.' "

"Not if he is going to hurt our people," Charisa said quickly.

Her father did not reply.

She knew from the way he pressed his lips together and the angle at which he held his chin that he was annoyed.

They were also the signs that he was ready to go into battle.

She thought it would be a very brave man who would defy her father when he was fighting for something he believed to be right.

They arrived at the Priory.

As they walked up the steps, the Marquis came into the hall to greet them.

"It is delightful to see you back," he said, "and after all, you will not be bored by me alone because two of my friends have just arrived from Paris! They are so looking forward to meeting you, and I know you will find them as amusing and interesting as I do."

He took them into the Drawing-Room, and Charisa saw there were two people there, a man and a woman.

As she walked towards the woman she thought she had never seen anyone so smart and at the same time so unusual.

"Ariste, my dear," the Marquis was saying, "may I introduce to you my lovely cousin, Charisa Templeton, and her father, Colonel Lionel Templeton, who has been helping me with my new responsibilities."

The lady held out her hand as the Marquis finished:

"*Madame* Ariste Dubus is one of my oldest and most cherished friends."

"I am enchanted to meet you!" *Madame* Dubus said to Charisa.

Looking up at the Colonel from under her long, dark eye-lashes, she said:

"And, of course, Colonel, Gervais has extolled your virtues, which I can see at a glance was undoubtedly justified."

She spoke good English, but with a definite accent.

She was not exactly pretty. At the same time, she had an allure that was inescapable.

Charisa was aware that the way she spoke and looked at her father was extremely flirtatious.

The Marquis then drew forward a young man.

"And here is another old friend," he said, "who is the same age as myself and has been almost like a brother to me. *Comte* Jean de Soisson and I were at school together, and of course we both left with flying colours!"

The *Comte* shook hands.

Then as *Madame* Dubus talked to the Colonel, he concentrated on Charisa.

"You are lovely!" he exclaimed. "You would conquer all Paris from the moment you set foot there!"

"I am quite happy to remain in England," Charisa replied, "although you may find it rather dull."

"Not if you are here," the *Comte* replied.

She thought the way he looked at her was somewhat bold.

She moved away from him towards her father.

He had, however, been swept across the room by *Madame* Dubus.

They were standing at the window and he was pointing out to her the beauty of the garden.

The Marquis was at the grog-tray, pouring out glasses of champagne.

Charisa had expected there would be tea.

Now she wondered if that was too English a meal for the Marquis.

Perhaps he had told Dawkins not to bring in the magnificent silver tray with its early Georgian kettle, teapot, milk-jug, and sugar basin.

In which case there would be no delicious scones, sandwiches, iced cakes, and brandy-snaps.

She had come to expect them as a feature of tea-time at the Priory.

Gervais came across the room, a glass of champagne in each hand.

"I am sure you need this, Jean," he said to the *Comte*, "and a glass will do you good, Charisa."

"Thank you, no," Charisa replied. "It is too early, and I would prefer a glass of lemonade."

"I think you are making a mistake," the

Comte said. "This is particularly fine vintage which I have just brought over from France at the request of my friend, Gervais, and it is well worth the large number of *francs* it cost!"

Charisa did not answer.

She was thinking that Gervais was so hard up and already trying to rely on her father.

It was therefore a mistake for him to spend a great deal of money on drink.

It was also the sort of thing that would be gossiped about in the village, and eventually in the County.

Madame Dubus was still talking in a confidential manner to the Colonel.

The Marquis brought Charisa her glass of lemonade and she sat down on the sofa.

The *Comte* joined her, sitting, she thought, rather nearer than was necessary.

"I have always known that English girls were beautiful," he said, "but now I am captivated, entranced, dazzled by one of the most beautiful women I have ever seen!"

"You can hardly expect me to believe that," Charisa replied, "when in England we are always told that Frenchwomen are more entrancing than any others in the world and certainly more *chic*."

"*Chic* is something you can acquire —

beauty is what you are born with," the *Comte* replied.

The Marquis, who was listening, laughed.

"That is good, Jean!" he said. "I have never known you at a loss for words, and what you say sounds even better in English than it does in French!"

"I assure you I could say even more ardent things to *Mademoiselle* in French," Jean replied, "if I was sure she understood them."

"If you are asking whether or not I speak French," Charisa replied a little coldly, "I can tell you that I am able to do so quite adequately."

Her mother had also insisted that she speak French with a Parisian accent.

"Then prove to me that your voice is even lovelier in my language than in your own," the *Comte* replied as if it were a challenge.

"I will speak in French merely in order to show you that you are not superior in being bi-lingual," Charisa said in French.

The *Comte* de Soisson laughed and clapped his hands.

"Bravo! That is magnificent! Now I know that I am not superior, but merely a humble supplicant at your feet!"

Charisa thought he was somewhat ridiculous.

Like Gervais, he was over-dressed and in a way too smart, especially for the country.

She was quite sure that the Mawde relatives would disapprove of him, not only as himself but even more as a friend of the head of the family.

Gervais was taking glasses of champagne to *Madame* Dubus and the Colonel.

Now they came back from the window to join the others round the fireplace.

"I see, my dear," the Colonel said to his daughter, "that you are being sensible in drinking lemonade rather than champagne. I feel ashamed at breaking my Regimental rule of no alcohol until the sun goes down!"

The *Comte* laughed.

"You English are always denying yourselves the things that are pleasant, amusing, and delicious simply because you are afraid of enjoying life to the full, as we do in France."

"It depends what you call enjoyment," the Colonel said a little heavily.

The *Comte* raised his glass.

"Let us start with wine and women," he said, "the rest comes naturally."

The Colonel smiled, but Charisa knew he was feeling a little out of his depth.

The *Comte* was talking as if he were giving a performance on the stage.

The same might be said of *Madame* Dubus.

She put her hand on the Colonel's arm as she said:

"Very soon, my dear English Colonel, you must come to Paris as my guest, and I will amuse you with delights which will be more exciting and more intriguing than anything you have ever dreamt of!"

Once again she was fluttering her long eye-lashes.

She was also pouting her lips in a manner which made it obvious that she wished to flirt with the Colonel.

They talked until Charisa said:

"I think I would like to go upstairs and have a little rest before dinner."

It was something she never did at home.

But she felt uncomfortable because of the way the *Comte* was looking at her.

She also disliked the intimate manner in which *Madame* Dubus was talking to her father.

She knew how it would have upset and shocked her mother, and she thought too that he was somewhat uneasy.

"I do not like these people!" she told herself. "I certainly hope the rest of the party will be different."

She knew that they would not fit in with

the rest of her family.

In fact, they would undoubtedly be shocked.

Madame Dubus was expostulating that she must not leave them, but the Marquis said:

"There is no hurry. Dinner will not be until half past eight, and that is very much earlier than if we were in Paris."

Charisa knew this was true, but she perceived it to be quite late by English standards.

However, she was too polite to say so.

She merely walked towards the door.

There was nothing the *Comte* could do but open it for her.

She went up the stairs.

She did not need to be told she would be in the room she always occupied at the Priory.

It was a room she particularly loved because it had been decorated by her mother.

She had been allowed to choose the curtains she wanted and some of the furniture.

Charisa had also begged the old Marquis to let her have a picture she loved above all others.

Even when she was very small she used to stand entranced in front of a painting by Louis Cranach.

She thought that "Rest on the Flight to Egypt" was the most beautiful and exciting picture she had ever seen.

It portrayed the Holy Child in the arms of Mary, His Mother, with Joseph standing behind them.

All around them flying and running over the ground were Angels with their wings out-stretched.

It had captured Charisa's imagination.

When the Marquis allowed her to have it in her bed-room she would lie in bed and look at it in the morning.

She also said her prayers to it at night.

The room itself was in the oldest part of the Priory.

The walls were covered in panelling which had been painted white.

Everything else in the room was in colours that blended with the Cranach picture.

The curtains were the deep blue of the Madonna's robe.

The pink, the blue, the colour of the ground on which Holy Family were resting, were all to be found in the exquisitely woven carpet.

The curtains of the bed fell from a golden corolla on which there were also Angels.

As she entered the room, Charisa saw that the gardeners had brought into the house for her all the flowers she loved.

There were lilies that had just come into bloom, vases of which stood on either side of the fireplace.

There were white roses on the Chest of Drawers.

It all looked as it always had whenever she came to the Priory.

The only exception was that on the dressing-table there was a vase of the same orchids that the Marquis had sent to her home.

As she looked at them she realised she had not thanked him.

It was something for which she must apologise when she went down to dinner.

She had come upstairs earlier than expected.

The elderly housemaid, Bessy, who usually looked after her, came bustling into the room, saying:

"I thinks as 'ow you were still downstairs, Miss Charisa, but it's nice to 'ave you in your own room again, an' no mistake!"

"It is nice to see you too, Bessy," Charisa said. "How are you?"

"Run orf me feet, Miss, an' that's the truth!" Bessy replied. "I don't know if I'm on me 'ead or me 'eels with everythin' done topsy-turvy from wot it's bin before."

"What do you mean by that?" Charisa asked as Bessy undid her gown.

"Breakfast at eleven o'clock so we can't get into the bed-rooms as we've always done," Bessy replied. "Lunch when 'alf the afternoon's gone, an' now it's dinner gettin' on for midnight!"

The way Bessy spoke was so funny that Charisa could only laugh.

"French times are different from ours."

"An' so are French folks!" Bessy said. "You should see the trunks th' lady as 'as come 'as brought with 'er. You'd think 'er'd come to stay for th' next five years!"

"I can see she is very smart!" Charisa said.

She could not help noticing even to herself that there was a cold note in her voice.

She had already decided that she did not like *Madame* Dubus.

She did not like the *Comte* de Soisson either.

Then she thought she was being very insular.

It was a great mistake not to expect foreigners to be different and not to appreciate the difference rather than disparage it.

Now she said to Bessy:

"I said I wanted to rest before dinner, but actually I thought it would be pleasant to be up here, read a book, and look at my picture."

"I thought you'd be wantin' to see that," Bessy smiled. " 'Miss Charisa's picture' is what us always calls it downstairs, an' very pretty it is too, what with all 'em small angels hoppin' about."

"I have loved it ever since I can remember," Charisa said, "and while I am here I am going to look at all the other pictures in the Gallery as if I had never seen them before."

"You'd better be quick about it then," Bessy said, " 'cause when you looks again, they might not be there!"

Charisa was still.

"What do you mean by that?"

Bessy lowered her voice.

"I 'ears 'Is Lordship's bin askin' Mr. Sheldon which are th' pictures that can be sold."

Charisa stared at her in astonishment.

"Sold?" she exclaimed. "But surely he knows they are all entailed like everything else in the house."

" 'Is Lordship apparently says: 'There must be some things that ain't on that damned Inventory!' "

As Bessy spoke, she put her fingers up to her lips.

"I'm sorry, Miss Charisa, but them's was 'Is Lordship's exac' words."

Mr. Sheldon ran both the house and the Estate.

Charisa was quite certain that if the Marquis had been talking to him, it had to be in private.

Everything he said had therefore been overheard by servants who were listening at key-holes.

It did not surprise her.

She knew that the servants would have been extremely curious about everything the new Marquis said and did.

At the same time, she was horrified that Gervais, so soon after his arrival, should be talking of selling anything.

She thought she would tell her father at once.

If it was a question of selling the pictures, he must make sure they were offered to him first.

Then she wondered why the Marquis wanted so much money.

Had he commitments in France, or was it just extravagance.

When Bessy had left her, she did not lie on the bed.

She stood at the window, looking out at the garden.

It was quite obvious why the Marquis wanted to marry her, also why he was already

hoping that her father would contin   ʽ
help finance the Estate, as he had in the

That he might sell the pictures, or a
the other treasures in the house, was something that would never have occurred to the
old Marquis.

It had certainly never occurred to any of
the previous Mawdes who had in turn inherited the Priory.

The house and everything in it had been a
sacred trust.

It had been passed on from one generation to the next all down the centuries.

They had at one time or another to de-
prive themselves of things like horses, a
house in London, and expensive entertain-
ments.

Charisa was, however, quite sure that
never for one moment had they thought
they could sell their heritage.

They must be passed on to the next heir in
the same state of perfection in which it had
come to them.

'Papa must stop him!' she thought.

Then she wondered if in fact it would be
possible for the Colonel to do so.

She moved from the window back into
the room to look up at her picture.

Just as she had as a child, she thought she
herself was one of the small Angels flying

...bout the Infant Jesus.

They were worshipping Him, and at the same time protecting Him.

"That is what you have to do now," she said, "protect the Priory and everything in it."

She had a sudden longing to pray, and she wished to be sure her prayers were heard.

Bessy had left her wearing a pretty *negligée* which matched the nightgown she had on.

She thought it would take her no more than a few minutes to slip downstairs to the Chapel.

She wanted to pray there as she had always done when she was staying at the Priory.

There were, in fact, two Chapels at Mawdelyn.

One was the big Chapel which had been built for the monks and which could hold a hundred people with ease.

Then there was a small Chapel which had been erected over the tomb of the first Abbot.

It was very small, in fact only about twelve people could worship there comfortably.

Because it was seldom used, Charisa, when she was staying at the Priory, nearly always prayed there.

She felt that the monks who still watched

over everything that happened in the Priory were glad the little Chapel was not forgotten.

It was easy for her now to slip along the wide corridor in which her bed-room was situated.

She walked down a small staircase at the end of the main building.

At the bottom of it there was a passage which led to the Chapel.

She reached it and opened the door.

The evening sun was coming through the beautiful stained-glass window.

The rest of the Chapel where there were no windows was in shadow.

There were no flowers as Charisa knew there would be in the big Chapel.

As she walked towards the altar the sun was in her eyes.

She felt that the golden light came from Heaven as if to welcome her.

She reached the altar steps and knelt down.

Then she looked up.

She was expecting to see the beautiful ancient gold Cross with jewels which was believed to have belonged personally to the first Abbot.

She could not see it.

Feeling it was because of the sun in her

eyes, she put up her hand to shade them.

Now she could see more clearly.

It was then she realised that the Cross had gone.

So had the six gold candlesticks that had always stood on either side of it.

chapter four

"He has sold them!"

Charisa gasped the words, and looked again as if she could not believe her eyes.

How was it possible that Gervais could have sold anything so precious, so completely unique to the Priory?

Abbot Mawdelyn had been christened after a fifteenth-century Saint who had performed a number of miracles during his lifetime.

But Charisa always thought the Abbot himself also was a Saint.

Connoisseurs frequently came to the Priory to admire the pictures and its other treasures.

They thought the Cross and the candlesticks had been a present to Abbot Mawdelyn.

It was difficult to pin-point exactly the year they had been made, but they were certainly of the right period.

There was no other Church or Chapel in the whole of England that possessed a finer decoration for its altar.

When Charisa was a child she would

watch the sunlight glinting on the jewels.

She believed they were telling her that her small prayers were heard.

Now to see the altar bare was a shock.

She wanted to cry because something so precious was missing.

As she knelt to pray, she wondered what she could do about it.

She knew it would upset her father, but he had no authority over Gervais.

He was not a Trustee of the Estate, although, of course, he could communicate with those who were.

He knew them well, but they were now very old men.

They could not be continually watching over the contents of the Priory to see that nothing was lost.

"What shall I do?"

She asked the question aloud, then realised it was a prayer.

Then, as she knelt there with the sunshine enveloping her, she had the feeling that her prayers were heard.

Not only that, but the Abbot himself was near to her.

She could not explain exactly what she felt, and yet she was conscious of a spiritual presence.

Strangely enough, she was sure that it was

warning her of danger.

She did not understand, but the warning was definitely there.

She could feel it just as she had felt the streak of repugnance when Gervais kissed her hand.

"What . . . can I . . . do?" she asked. "Tell me . . . what I can . . . do?"

She tried to listen with her heart as her mother had taught her to do.

"When God speaks," Mrs. Templeton had said, " we do not hear it with our ears as we hear human voices, we hear it within ourselves. It is really the voice of our Soul."

"Help me . . . please help me . . ." Charisa prayed now.

She felt to her surprise that the Abbot was telling her that for the moment she should do nothing.

"But surely Papa could persuade him not to sell anything so priceless?" she argued in her mind.

Again the warning was there.

There was danger, and she was to do nothing, just be prepared and, of course, pray.

She did not understand.

She covered her face with her hands as if to blot out the sun.

She prayed insistently with her whole

being that the Priory would not be hurt, that it would be as beautifully holy as it had always been.

Then, as she finished her prayer, she knew that the spirit of the Abbot, which had been beside her, had gone.

The sunshine, however, still enveloped her and, strangely, she felt happy.

'Perhaps it will be . . . all right,' she thought a little doubtfully.

Slowly she rose from her knees and walked down the short aisle past the ancient pews.

As she reached the door, she turned to look back.

The altar was still enveloped with a golden haze.

She thought that God had sent the sunshine to take the place of the Cross and the candlesticks as if to reassure her that He was watching over the Priory.

Charisa stood for a long time just looking at the altar.

Then slowly she went up the stairs and back to her bed-room.

Only when she lay on the bed did she realise that she had had a very strange experience.

It was something she thought she would always remember.

She wanted to tell her father about it, but if she did so, she knew it would worry him.

He would be horrified at the disappearance of the Cross and the candlesticks.

She was sure, moreover, that the Abbot wanted her to keep it a secret to herself.

'It was all very strange,' she thought.

At the same time, she felt she had been blessed.

Of one thing she was quite certain — the Abbot and the monks were watching over the Priory.

The next morning the sun was shining.

Charisa knew it was going to be a very hot day.

She remembered that Gervais had said he wanted her to go riding with him.

She therefore put on one of her light summer riding-habits before she went down to breakfast.

She was not surprised when she entered the Breakfast-Room to find the only person present was her father.

"Good-morning, my dearest!" the Colonel said. "I think we are alone. Dawkins told me that *Madame* will be breakfasting upstairs, and our host has not yet even been called."

Charisa laughed.

"It seems strange for anyone in England to wake so late," she said, "but I expect

Gervais is used to the gaieties of Paris, which I understand go on until dawn."

She thought her father looked disapproving, and quickly changed the subject to horses.

"Gervais did say he wanted to ride with me," she said. "Which horse would you recommend for him and, more important, which one for me?"

Her father instantly started to describe what he thought were the outstanding qualities of the horses he had bought for the Marquis just before his death.

They had arrived only that week.

"I wish Vincent were alive," he remarked. "He was a magnificent rider — one of the best I have ever seen."

Charisa made a little murmur of agreement, and her father went on:

"I always thought that one day, when he left the Army and took his rightful place here, we would build a Race-Course."

He paused and then continued:

"It is something which is very much needed in this part of the country, and I would enjoy it myself."

"What a wonderful idea, Papa!" Charisa said. "Perhaps it is something Gervais also would enjoy."

"I doubt that," her father replied. "He is a 'Park Rider,' and would not be an experienced jumper. And I have the feeling, although I may be wrong, that he is not really a very enthusiastic horseman."

Charisa looked at her father in consternation.

"I hope that is not true! What would the Priory be like without its stables and outstanding horses?"

As she spoke, she wondered if Gervais would sell the horses if he needed money.

Because the idea perturbed her, she said to her father:

"I was wondering, Papa, if you are really going to help Gervais financially. It seems he can hardly manage without you."

There was silence while the Colonel obviously thought about what he should reply.

Then he said:

"I have not the faintest idea of what Gervais wants to spend money on, and to be honest, after what Matthews said to me, I have no intention of giving him a blank cheque."

"I know what you mean, Papa," Charisa said in a low voice, "and I am sure you are right."

She was just about to say more when the door opened and the *Comte* came in.

"Good-morning!" he said. "I see I am late, but do not be cross with me. The sun is shining, and *Mademoiselle* looks even more beautiful than she did last night!"

"There is no hurry," Charisa said. "I expected to go riding with Gervais, but I hear he has not yet been called."

"I think he is likely to sleep until midday," the *Comte* replied, "so you must allow me to take his place. I am looking forward to seeing the horses."

He glanced at the Colonel before he went on:

"I am told that your father contributed to them as well as to some of the other delightful possessions which Gervais has been lucky enough to inherit."

"Who told you that?" the Colonel asked sharply.

"Gervais, of course," the *Comte* replied, "and I know how grateful he is to you for your kindness to his uncle."

The *Comte* spread out his hands in a typically French gesture as he added:

"Can you imagine what it was like for him to learn that he was heir to this magnificent house, its contents, and vast Estates?"

"I can understand that he was delighted!" Charisa said a little coldly.

" 'Delighted' is hardly the word!" the *Comte* said. "It saved him from virtual starvation. He jumped so high with joy that I thought he would touch the moon!"

Charisa thought it would be more becoming if Gervais had at least expressed some sort of regret at his uncle's death.

After all, the Marquis had always been very kind to him, paying his debts over and over again.

"It was very fortunate for Gervais," the *Comte* continued as if he were a little envious, "that his cousin should have been killed in India. One might almost say it was a remarkable coincidence that he should have died so conveniently when Gervais was at his wit's end."

"I was very fond of Vincent," Charisa said quietly, "as was everybody in the house and in the village. They wept bitterly when they heard the sad news."

"You have a saying in England, I think," the *Comte* replied. " 'It is an ill wind that blows nobody any good.' Gervais is a very lucky chap!"

There was no doubt now of the envious note in his voice.

Charisa, although she had not finished her breakfast, got up from the table.

"Shall we go and look at the new horses, Papa?" she asked. "I know you have a lot to tell me about them."

"Will you not wait for me, Beautiful Lady?" the *Comte* pleaded. "I want to see you riding like an Amazon or, should I say, like a goddess."

"I think we should wait until our host appears," Charisa said. "In the meantime, Papa and I will not be riding, but just looking at the horses."

She walked from the room as she spoke, and her father followed her.

As he shut the door so that he could not be overheard, he said in a low voice:

"Insolent young puppy! He has no right to talk to you in that familiar manner!"

"I quite agree," Charisa said, "and I thought it was very bad manners to talk as he did about Gervais when he is his guest."

"Why must we have all these foreigners in the Priory, of all places?" the Colonel asked beneath his breath.

Charisa did not reply.

She knew as they walked towards the stables that he was thinking about Vincent, just as she was.

She could remember only too well how brilliantly he rode.

And yet he had always been very kind to her when they went riding together.

He would not allow her to take jumps that were too high for the horses on which she was riding.

He would always wait for her if his mount

was faster than hers.

She was sure that her father was right, and that Gervais and the *Comte* were only "Park Riders."

That meant that three-quarters of the well-bred horses, many of them with an Arab strain in them, would be wasted.

She wondered if she should suggest to her father that Gervais might sell the horses, and that he should buy them.

It seemed somewhat ironic when he had bought them for the Marquis in the first place.

But she could not bear to think of their being scattered.

Perhaps they would go to owners who did not appreciate how fine they were or might even be cruel to them.

She knew that her father would never sell a horse without knowing its owner and being certain the new owner would be as careful with the animal as he had been.

Once again, almost as if she could feel him beside her, she thought the Abbot was telling her to remain silent.

But for what reason, she could not understand.

She and her father spent a happy time in the stables going from stall to stall with the Head Groom.

They made a fuss of the horses, going over their finer points as they had often done before.

It was an hour and a half later before they were joined by Gervais and the *Comte*.

They were both looking excessively smart, too smart for a ride in the country, where no one would see them.

The best horses were brought out first for their inspection.

Then they set off.

They went first to the gallop which was just behind the Priory.

Charisa had to admit that Gervais looked very well on a horse and so did the *Comte*.

But they both refused to jump the hedges into the next field.

When the Colonel and Charisa did so, they always made an excuse.

Gervais wanted to "get to know" his horses before he did anything spectacular.

The *Comte* said he was not in the mood for being too energetic.

Finally they rode home after looking at one of the farms which Gervais had not seen before.

As they did so, Charisa knew she was right about him.

He rode only because it was the thing to do.

He enjoyed the admiration he would receive if an audience was present.

Otherwise, riding meant very little to him.

He had, in fact, shown more interest in the farm than anything else.

He wanted to know what profit it was making, and if they were cultivating enough land to make sure of a good harvest.

The Colonel answered his questions.

At the same time, Charisa was well aware that her father was not happy.

When they returned to the Priory, *Madame* Dubus was downstairs.

She was looking even smarter and more elegant than she had done yesterday.

Yet her red lips and mascaraed eye-lashes looked out-of-place in the Priory.

She met them in the hall.

She kissed Gervais and the *Comte* affectionately before she greeted the Colonel.

"I missed through sheer laziness seeing you ride, my dear Colonel," she said, "but it is something I will not neglect to do another day, for I have been told how magnificent you look on a horse!"

She was flirting with him again.

Before the Colonel could reply, she said to Gervais:

"I have news for you, *mon brave*. Our friends are arriving to-morrow. I know how pleased you will be."

"All of them?" Gervais asked.

"*All* of them!" *Madame* Dubus confirmed.

Listening, Charisa knew that the way she emphasised her words had a special meaning for Gervais.

She thought, too, that his dark eyes lit up with a strange excitement.

"They will be very, very welcome," he said.

Madame Dubus smiled.

"That is what I thought you would say."

They moved into the Salon which was next to the Dining-Room.

There was a bottle of champagne in the ice-cooler.

Charisa was not surprised.

At the same time, she thought it strange that anyone should want to drink so early when they were in the country.

Her father accepted a glass as if he thought it would be somewhat churlish to refuse.

She noticed he sipped only a very little of it, then put it down on a side-table, where it would not be noticed.

Madame Dubus was talking to him in her usual intimate manner.

Because she suddenly disliked the whole

thing, Charisa went up to her bed-room to take off her riding-clothes.

In the afternoon Charisa expected they would go driving.

Gervais, however, said it was too hot.

She therefore left the party and went up to the Picture Gallery.

She was half-afraid she would see gaps where some of the pictures had been removed.

To her relief, they were all there.

She thought even Gervais would not dare to sell a treasure that was entailed.

She knew her father had a copy of the inventory of the contents of the Priory.

She had never bothered to examine it at all closely.

She had always thought of everything as being a part of the place, and there could never be a suggestion of anything being removed, let alone sold.

She was looking at a particularly fine portrait of the 2nd Marquis by Van Dyck, when she heard someone approaching the Gallery.

She looked round, hoping it was her father, but it was Gervais coming towards her.

When he reached her side she said, not looking at him:

"I was just admiring this wonderful portrait by Van Dyck of the Marquis who brought to the Priory Louis XVI furniture from Versailles."

"I wondered why so many of the things seemed familiar!" Gervais exclaimed.

Charisa looked at him in astonishment.

"Surely you have read the history of the Mawdes?" she asked. "There are several different accounts, but much the best is one which came out fifteen years ago."

"I suppose I ought to read it some time," Gervais said casually.

"You ought to read it now — at once!" Charisa exclaimed. "After all, you can be very proud of your antecedents. And there is a story attached to almost everything in this house."

"I think it is your duty to teach me what I ought to know," Gervais replied. "How soon, Charisa, are you going to marry me?"

Too late Charisa remembered that she had told herself she must be careful never to be alone with him.

This was what she had wanted to avoid.

Now it was too late to run away.

"I am very honoured that you should ask me," she managed to reply. "At the same time, we have only just met each other, and I would not think of marrying anyone unless

I knew him very well."

"You know about my ancestry, and I am very well aware how much the family means to you, and of course the Priory," Gervais said. "So what are we waiting for?"

"It is hard to put it into words," Charisa answered, "but it is . . . that I should . . . love you."

"I will make you love me," Gervais said. "There will be no difficulty about that, and think how much you will enjoy running this house and spending your money to make it finer than it is at the moment."

Charisa did not answer.

Then, unexpectedly, he put his arms around her.

"You will love me," he said, "and we will be very happy!"

At his touch she felt the same streak of repugnance that had upset her when he had kissed her hand.

It swept through her whole body.

She had turned her face away from him, but before she could struggle free, his lips were on her cheek.

It was not lightning that now seemed to sweep through her, but the cut of a knife.

It was so sharp, so painful, that she actually gave a little scream of terror.

She fought against Gervais so violently

that it took him by surprise.

Before he could prevent her, she was free and running down the Gallery.

It was as if the Devil himself were pursuing her.

"Charisa! Charisa!" he called.

But by this time she was tearing down the corridor which led to the stairs.

She went up them so quickly that by the time Gervais reached the door of the Gallery, she had disappeared.

She ran into her bed-room and locked the door behind her.

It was then she realised she was breathless and trembling.

She sat down on her bed and put her hands on her breasts.

She was trying to soothe the tumult within them.

"Why does he make me feel like this?" she asked herself.

She could not explain the sheer horror Gervais evoked when he touched her, or the intensity of it.

When she had been in London, Charisa had received three proposals of marriage.

She had refused them all, but she hated to be so unkind.

She was well aware that in one instance, at any rate, it was her fortune that had counted more than anything else.

At the same time, there had been a note of sincerity even in that man's voice.

She thought he was also in love with her as a person.

The other two men had been genuinely in love, and she had tried to be as gentle as possible.

She told them that what she felt for them was friendship.

She hoped never to lose them.

But it was not love, and for marriage that was essential.

Where Gervais was concerned, she knew now that she hated him.

The feeling of repugnance she had when he touched her was so strong that she found it unbearable even to be close to him.

'There is something wrong . . . very . . . wrong,' she thought.

At the same time, she was slightly ashamed at being hysterical about it.

Having tidied her hair, she forced herself to go downstairs to find her father.

As she expected, he was still being monopolised by *Madame* Dubus.

She therefore challenged the *Comte* to Backgammon.

He was only too pleased to play with her.

When later Gervais came back into the

Salon, there was a look in his eyes Charisa did not understand.

When she had refused other men, they had looked at her pleadingly.

They obviously hoped she would change her mind.

But she had the uncomfortable feeling there was something hard in Gervais's expression.

She felt he was determined to have his own way.

To save herself, she would have to fight.

'The sooner we leave the Priory, the better!' she thought.

She decided she must speak to her father about it.

Unfortunately, she did not get the chance before they went up to dress for dinner.

She learnt only just before they did so that a number of other guests had been invited.

There was nobody exciting, just members of the Mawde family over whom Gervais was making a tremendous fuss.

He seemed to beguile them in a way that gave them confidence in him.

He asked their help.

He obviously was trying to make them think he was the most charming and pleasant head of the family it was possible for them to have.

When the Ladies left the Gentlemen, one of Gervais's aunts said to Charisa:

"I am very upset, dear child, to learn how impoverished poor, dear Gervais is."

"Did he tell you that?" Charisa asked.

"Yes, he did," the aunt replied, "but you do understand, my dear, that if he cannot afford to make me the allowance I have always had, I do not know how I shall be able to manage."

Charisa knew that it was traditional, as in most great families, for the Marquis to control most of the money.

He gave allowances to most of his relatives, especially those who were widowed or unmarried.

She knew it was one of the reasons the last Marquis had relied so tremendously on her father.

She could not help feeling this would be another weighty argument Gervais would use to compel her to marry him.

However, she could not bear to see the old aunt so upset.

So she put her hand over hers as she said:

"Do not worry. I will talk to Papa and see if he can make Gervais understand the position better than he does at the moment."

It made her angry to think that Gervais was spending so much on wine and champagne.

He was also doubtless paying the fares for his friends from Paris.

He would entertain them royally while threatening to cut down the not very large allowances his relatives had been receiving.

When she counted them up, she realised despairingly that there were about twenty elderly men and women who were dependent on him.

They would suffer acutely if he told them they could no longer expect the allowance they had received year after year from his uncle.

'I must talk to Papa,' she thought.

But it seemed impossible to get him alone.

Finally, when the dinner-party broke up and the guests were leaving, she went upstairs.

She knew she had to think out exactly what she should say to her father.

Yet she had the strange feeling that the Abbot was still telling her to keep silent.

Why he should do so, she still had no idea.

Before she got into bed she pulled back the curtains over the window to look up at the stars.

"Help me! Help me!" she whispered.

She was not certain whether she was praying to the Abbot or to her mother.

She left the curtains undrawn.

The moonlight was very lovely and soothing as it illuminated the room.

In bed she looked up at the stars.

As they shone like the Star of Bethlehem she prayed for the troubles that seemed to be encroaching on her one by one.

Charisa had fallen asleep and was dreaming when she heard a voice say:

"Charisa!"

It was part of her dream — and yet it came again.

"Charisa — wake up!"

She opened her eyes and saw a man's head silhouetted against the moonlight.

Sleepily, she thought it must be her father.

Then the voice said:

"Do not be frightened, Charisa. It is Vincent!"

Still half asleep, she said:

"Vincent . . . is . . . dead."

As she spoke, she opened her eyes.

The man was sitting on her bed looking down at her, and he replied:

"No, Charisa, I am alive!"

For a moment she could only stare.

Then she gave a cry.

"Vincent! Is it . . . really . . . you?"

"It is me, and I am alive!"

Charisa sat up.

Then she flung her arms around Vincent's neck and hugged him as she had done as a child.

"Vincent! Vincent! Can it . . . really be . . . true?"

His arms went round her and he held her close.

"It is true!" he said. "And Charisa, I need your help! I need it desperately!"

Charisa's cheek was against his.

"They . . . said you were . . . dead," she said. "Oh, Vincent, why did . . . they think . . . you were . . . dead?"

"That is what I am going to explain to you," he answered.

He held her a little away from him and saw the tears running down her cheek.

They were tears of happiness because he was there and alive.

He took a handkerchief from his pocket and wiped her eyes very gently.

"When I saw you were in this room," he said, "it was just what I wanted! I was wondering how I could get in touch with you."

"H-how did you . . . how did you . . . get in?" Charisa asked.

Then before he could answer she gave an exclamation.

"You came . . . through the . . . secret passages!"

"Yes, of course!" he answered.

She wiped the remaining tears from her eyes with her fingers.

"Tell me what has happened."

Then she gave another cry.

"Oh, Vincent . . . then you are . . . the real . . . Marquis and . . . Gervais is making such a . . . mess of everything!"

"I thought he would," Vincent said grimly. "But before I tell you the whole story, Charisa — I have a lot to say — could you possibly find me something to eat?"

Charisa stared at him.

"You are . . . hungry?"

"I ran out of money and have had nothing to eat since yesterday."

Charisa gave a gasp of horror.

"I will go and get you something," she said. "In the meantime . . ."

She reached out towards the table beside her bed.

At the Priory Mrs. Bush always put a bottle of fresh water beside every guest's bed.

There was also a small tin containing biscuits in case they felt hungry in the night.

Charisa handed the tin to Vincent.

Without saying anything, he opened it

and started to eat the biscuits, not greedily, but as if he savoured every mouthful.

"I will go and find you some food," she said.

"For God's sake, do not let anybody realise I am here!" he said.

"Why not?"

"That is what I am going to explain to you."

Charisa got out of bed and crossed the room.

Her *negligée* was lying on a chair.

For a moment her body in the thin night-gown was silhouetted against the moonlight.

Vincent realised that while he had been thinking of her as the child he had left behind, she was now very much a woman.

As Charisa buttoned up her *negligée* she said:

"I will not be long. No one will come in, but if you feel afraid they might, lock the door."

"If it is anyone but you," Vincent replied, "I will go back into the secret passage."

She smiled at him before she went from the room.

She was feeling as if her head were in a whirl.

How was it possible that Vincent was alive and why was he in hiding?

118

She was so curious that she could hardly bear to go downstairs and leave him.

At the same time, in the glimpse she had of him in the moonlight he looked very different from how she remembered him.

He was wearing a shirt that was open at the neck.

Even in the quick glance he seemed to be almost in rags.

He wore no coat and she thought a bare knee was protruding through his trousers.

'What had happened? Why is he in such a state?' she asked.

Then she knew she must concentrate on finding him something to eat.

Like a ghost she moved bare-foot over the soft carpet to the far end of the corridor.

Then she went down a small staircase which she knew would lead her to the kitchens.

Everybody was asleep.

There was, however, one dangerous moment when she had to pass the Pantry.

One of the footmen always slept by the safe which contained the silver.

As she neared it, moving slowly just in case anyone was about, Charisa could hear him snoring.

Re-assured, she went down the flagged passage which led her to the kitchens.

They were very large and old.

They had been built so that food could be cooked for at least fifty monks several times a day.

Everything here was very quiet.

Although the flagstones which had been scrubbed clean were cold beneath Charisa's feet, she moved on.

She made her way to where beyond the kitchens the Larders were.

There had always been huge open bowls in there holding milk which was turning to cream.

The Larders were lower than ground level so that they were cool in all weathers.

There were slabs on which the food stood.

They were made of marble which had been put there centuries ago.

The windows were uncurtained, and in the moonlight it was easy for Charisa to find what she sought.

She found her way to where the serving plates were kept.

They were near the door beside which were also the carving-knives and forks.

Picking up a plate, she went first to where she could see there was the remains of a salmon.

It was what had been served at dinner.

Thinking quickly, she knew it would be a

mistake to take much of any one dish.

Mrs. Jones had been the Cook at the Priory ever since she could remember.

She had a keen eye and might accuse one of the kitchen-staff of helping themselves.

Charisa cut a large slice of the salmon.

She then took two slices of ox-tongue which she remembered seeing on the side-board at breakfast-time.

She also cut two slices of home-cured ham.

A joint of meat which she suspected had been served for supper in the Servants' Hall provided several more slices.

She felt sure what she took would not be missed.

On another slab there was a bowl of mixed salad and what was left of the sauce which went with it.

By this time the plate was nearly full.

She went towards the door, stopping only to pick up half a cottage loaf.

It had been baked early that morning, and she added a large pat of butter.

This had been made at the Priory and the Marquis's crest had been stamped on it.

Cautiously, because she was taking no chances, Charisa opened the door of the Larder.

Everything was silent as she started to walk back over the cold flagstones.

She had nearly reached the Dining-Room when she heard the footman still snoring in the Pantry.

It was then she thought there might be something left of the wines which had been passed round at dinner.

There had been champagne which they had also drunk in the Salon.

There had been what she knew was an excellent and expensive white wine and a vintage claret.

She was aware that during the late Marquis's illness and earlier, when he was not well the cellars had not been replenished.

She was therefore certain so much wine was sheer extravagance on Gervais's part.

She peeped into the Dining-Room.

As she had expected, there were a number of half-empty bottles standing on the sideboard.

There were also some clean knives and forks on it.

She put two on the plate and picked up a bottle of claret.

It was about three-quarters full, which was all she could safely carry.

Slowly, because both the plate and the bottle were heavy, she went up the stairs down which she had just come.

She was being careful not to trip over the front of her *negligée*.

It would not only make a noise but would also be a disaster when Vincent was so hungry.

Now she could think about him again.

It was almost impossible to realise he was really there and not dead.

She hurried down the passage because she was so thrilled at being able to go back to him.

When she reached her bed-room door she was just about to put down the bottle so as to open it, when it was opened from inside.

Vincent was there and she went in.

He did not speak until he had shut the door behind her, when he said:

"I was getting worried because you took so long. You did not see anybody?"

"Nobody saw me," Charisa said, "and I have brought you enough so that at least you will not feel hungry until to-morrow."

Vincent took the plate from her.

"You are a wonderful girl!" he said. "I will tell you just how wonderful after I have eaten everything you have brought me!"

He put the plate down on the table by the window.

There was a bowl of roses on it, which he pushed to one side.

He sat down in a chair and started to eat as she went to the bed-side table to fetch a glass.

She noticed as she did so that the biscuit-tin was empty.

She put the glass beside him and poured out the claret.

"I am not going to thank you," he said, "I am going to eat, then I am going to tell you everything you want to know."

"I am quite prepared to wait," Charisa said as she smiled.

As she spoke, she went back across the room and turned the key in the lock.

She thought as she did so that it was a strange thing to have to do in the Priory, of all places.

Then she remembered that when she was in the small Chapel, she had been aware that there was danger.

Now she realised that it did not apply to herself, but to Vincent.

Although she had not understood, she knew now that was why the Abbot had warned her.

It was Vincent who was in danger.

Vincent, who was supposed to be dead, but who had come home.

chapter five

Vincent put down his knife and fork.

"I do not think I have ever enjoyed a meal so much!" he exclaimed.

Charisa laughed before she said in a serious tone:

"I hope we do not have to decide how to get you many more!"

She was sitting against the pillows.

Vincent rose from the table and walked to the bed.

He sat down on it as he had before.

"Now," he said, "I am going to tell you exactly what has happened, but I do not want you to be frightened."

"Frightened?" she questioned.

She thought he would explain.

Instead, he began very carefully, as if he were choosing his words one by one, to tell her what had happened in India.

He related first how a young Officer had been stabbed in the back when he was in the Bazaar.

It was not until later that it had struck him that the knife was meant for him.

He skipped over what he was doing in

disguise in the North.

She learnt only that he was on his way back when Nicolas had joined him.

Charisa was listening.

Her hands were clasped in front of her.

Her large eyes were on Vincent's face, which she could see quite clearly in the moonlight.

She realised he was very thin.

There were lines on his face which had not been there when he left England.

He then related how Nicolas had told him of a brother Officer, who had moved into his bed when he had left the Barracks, had been killed.

Charisa made a little murmur of horror.

Then Vincent went on to explain how he had gone to the stream to fetch the beer he was keeping cool there.

When he returned to his tent, he found that Nicolas had been murdered.

As if she wanted somehow to protect him, Charisa put out her hand.

Vincent took it in both of his.

"I do not want to upset you," he said, "but I need your help and there is no one else I can trust."

"You . . . know I will . . . help you," Charisa answered, "but, Vincent . . . who could . . . want to . . . kill you?"

126

Vincent was silent.

Suddenly Charisa gave a cry that was almost a scream.

"It is Gervais! Of course — it is Gervais!"

"Why should you think that?" Vincent asked quietly.

"Because his friend the *Comte* Jean de Soisson, who arrived yesterday, told me that Gervais 'jumped for joy' when he learnt that Uncle George was dead."

She paused before she went on:

"The *Comte* said he was so excited that he might have jumped over the moon!"

Vincent looked at her but was still silent as she said, the words tumbling out of her mouth:

"Do . . . you not . . . see? You have . . . just told me that . . . Nicolas brought you . . . the newspaper in which it . . . was reported that your Uncle George was . . . dead. Gervais knew that when he . . . died he would be the next . . . Marquis! He could have . . . known that only if he had . . . disposed of you . . . !"

Vincent's hands tightened on hers.

"You are a very clever girl," he said, "as you always were. I knew when Nicolas told me of the death of my brother Officer that it was Gervais who was trying to kill me. That is why I came home at once, secretly and without anybody knowing who I was."

"How did you . . . do that?" Charisa asked.

She knew as she looked at the rags he was wearing that it could not have been a comfortable journey.

"I travelled in a cargo ship," Vincent explained, "and worked my passage back to England."

"It must have been awful!" Charisa exclaimed. "And when they found Nicolas's body, they must have thought it was you."

"I made sure of that," Vincent replied, "when I realised he was dead. I knew too there was nothing I could do but disappear."

"Why were they so sure the dead man was you?"

"Because it was so hot," Vincent explained, "Nicolas had taken off his uniform and was wearing only a pair of white pants. I took all his belongings, including his boots, and buried them under the trees."

There was pain in his voice as he spoke.

"Then I let my horse loose," he went on. "I was sure somebody would take care of him until the Army turned up to claim him."

"And you . . . rode away on your . . . friend's horse," Charisa said, trying to work it out.

"I did, but of course in a different direction from the one I would otherwise have taken. There was nothing left to identify Nicolas."

He paused and then continued:

"I knew that by the time he was found, the heat of the sun would have made it impossible to recognise anyone with certainty. But it was known that I was expected to be in that particular vicinity."

"I think it was very clever of you," Charisa said, "and that is exactly what happened. When he went to the War Office, Papa was told there was another Officer missing who they hoped could give them some information about you."

"By that time," Vincent said, "I was making for the coast. I was fortunate to find a cargo ship that was leaving for England. But the food was ghastly and the conditions on board were worse!"

"Poor Vincent! It must have been horrible!" Charisa said.

"The small wages I received for my toil," Vincent went on, "lasted me only until I was about thirty miles from here, and after that I had to walk."

"And you could not afford to buy any food," Charisa finished.

"I ate what I could find in the fields and on the trees," Vincent replied. "I really was starving when I saw the Priory in front of me."

"Yet you got here!" Charisa said softly.

"I slipped in through a side door and as quickly as possible crept into the secret passages," Vincent said.

"That was sensible," Charisa murmured.

"I had been thinking as I was walking along that the only person who would be able to help me was you. When I realised by peeping into the room that you were in the Priory, it seemed the answer to my prayers!"

"And I was thinking I should leave here as soon as possible," Charisa said. "Oh, Vincent, I am so very, very glad I am here!"

"So am I," he said, "but I am terrified in case I put you in any danger."

"You need not worry about that," Charisa said. "Gervais will not kill me."

"Why are you so sure about that?" Vincent asked sharply.

"Because he wants to marry me!"

Vincent stared at her in astonishment.

"You mean he has said that already? But, surely, he can only just have arrived."

"He went to London first," Charisa answered, "but as soon as he got here, he talked to Papa and intimated that he should marry me."

"I have never heard such damned impertinence!" Vincent exclaimed. "What did your father say?"

Charisa was silent for a moment.

"Good God," Vincent exclaimed, "you are not thinking of marrying him?"

"No, of course not," Charisa said, "and I knew he was evil and wicked from the moment he touched me."

"He touched you?" Vincent interrupted.

"He kissed my hand, and it was horrible, repulsive, and I knew there was something wrong."

"He is a murderer, for one thing!" Vincent said. "But you understand, Charisa, that anyone connected with me is in danger. That is why I did not go to your father."

"You mean . . . he might kill Papa?" Charisa said in a low voice.

"I think he would kill anybody who stood between him and the position he has now taken," Vincent said. "Three men have died already because they were thought to be me, but unless I am actually killed too, it is impossible to prove that he murdered them."

"But we have to prove it!" Charisa declared.

"Not until I am lying dead at his feet!" Vincent said grimly.

Charisa gave a cry of horror and held tightly to his hand.

"That must not happen! We cannot lose you, Vincent, and somehow we must get rid of Gervais."

Vincent sighed.

"I know that, but it is easier said than done. We will just have to wait and see what happens."

"And meanwhile you are going to hide in the secret passages?"

"It is the only place I will be safe," Vincent said, "and perhaps by some lucky chance I shall find some evidence that I can take to the Police."

He drew in his breath before he said very quietly:

"But you do understand that if he knows I am alive, he will kill me, and this time make sure of being successful."

"But . . . he cannot be . . . he must not! Oh, Vincent . . . I am frightened!" Charisa cried.

"I do not want to frighten you," Vincent said, "but if you can just keep me alive while I try to find proof that he is a murderer and an imposter, that is all I ask."

"You know I will do . . . anything to help . . . you," Charisa said, "just as I used to when we were children."

Vincent smiled.

"You always aided and abetted me in anything I wanted to do."

"That is what I will do . . . now," Charisa promised. "But, Vincent . . . dear Vincent, we must be very, very . . . careful."

"That is what I intend to be," he said, "and I shall be quite safe in the Priest's Hole."

The Priest's Hole was in the centre of the secret passages.

It had been used as a Chapel where Mass could be celebrated in secret.

It was also where the Priest could hide when he was being pursued.

It was, Charisa knew, safe.

No one was supposed to know the way to the secret passages except the immediate family.

But Vincent had shown them to Charisa when she was ten.

He had taken her into them many times in the next five years before he went abroad.

"If you are going to sleep in the Priest's Hole," she said, "you will need a pillow and blankets."

She stopped and exclaimed:

"Of course! There is no reason why you should not sleep in your own room."

Vincent stared at her.

"Why do you say that?"

"When I was talking to Bessy and saying how glad I was to be in my own room with the picture I love so much, Bessy said: 'Mrs. Bush'd never put you anywhere 'cept where you belongs, Miss Charisa, an' Mr. Dawkins has locked Mr. Vincent's room, which is just as t'were when 'e left it.' "

Vincent smiled.

"If Dawkins has the key," he said, "it means that no one can enter it unexpectedly, and, as you know, there is a secret entrance into my room as there is into yours."

"You can sleep in your own bed," Charisa said, "but be careful to leave it tidy in the morning. And of course your clothes are in the cupboards, just as you left them."

"I am certainly glad to hear that!" Vincent replied. "If nothing else, I need a new pair of shoes after walking all that way."

"You need some other things as well!" Charisa laughed.

"I know that," he said, "but at least no one tried to rob me!"

He spoke lightly, but Charisa said in a serious voice:

"No one but Gervais, who has . . . taken your . . . place!"

"I suppose he was hard up as usual," Vincent said angrily. "Uncle George was horrified at his extravagance."

"Getting rid of you was the only way he

could inherit the Priory," Charisa said, "and, Vincent, he is already trying to find things to sell."

"To sell?" Vincent exclaimed.

"He was overheard by the servants asking Mr. Sheldon which of the pictures were not entailed, and I think he has sold the gold Cross and the candlesticks from the altar of the Abbot's Chapel."

"Curse him!" Vincent exclaimed. "How dare he try to spoil the Priory!"

He got to his feet and walked to the window.

He stood looking out, but Charisa knew he was controlling his anger at what he had just heard.

She did not speak, and after some seconds Vincent came back to the bedside.

"You must get some sleep," he said. "Thanks to what you have just told me, I can sleep in my own room. But I shall be vigilant just in case anyone comes in and finds me there."

"I do not think they will do that," Charisa said. "At the same time, you must be very . . . very . . . careful."

"I will be," Vincent promised, "and you must be even more careful. We are dealing not with anyone who is normal, but like a desperate rake he will fight to the last ditch to keep what is legally not his."

"I know," Charisa said, "and I shall pray that you will be safe."

She hesitated before she said a little shyly:

"I think it is because everybody loves you so much and was so distressed by the news of your death that . . . God has brought . . . you safely . . . home!"

"I think you are right," Vincent said quietly, "and I am a very lucky man to have you to help me."

He bent towards her, and Charisa held out her arms to put them round his neck unaffectedly as she had done before.

She hugged him, and as she did so she said:

"How can you not be safe, here in your own home, when I know not only the monks but also Abbot Mawdelyn will be looking after you?"

Vincent kissed her cheek.

"And so are you, my dear little cousin," he said, "but remember — not a word to anyone!"

"No, of course not," Charisa agreed, "but I would like to tell Papa sometime. I know he would want to help to expose Gervais."

"You must not risk his life or anybody else's," Vincent said, "not for a moment."

He kissed her cheek again, then began to

move across the room.

Charisa gave a little cry.

"You have forgotten breakfast! I will get you some, but how shall I let you know when it is ready?"

Vincent thought for a moment.

"What time are you being called?" he asked.

"At eight o'clock," Charisa answered, "and I shall be in the Breakfast-Room at half-past-eight. Usually no one is downstairs except Papa and myself."

"Then if you come up here after breakfast, I will be waiting on the other side of your secret entrance. Remember, the housemaids will be about, so I will open it just wide enough for you to put the food, if you have any, inside. And remember not to speak."

"But I . . . have to talk . . . to you . . . and supposing I have . . . found out something . . . important to . . . tell you?"

"You can leave a piece of paper, a handkerchief, or anything that belongs to you just inside the panel," Vincent answered. "I will come here several times a day or, if you like, every two hours or so, just in case you need me."

Charisa gave a little sigh of relief.

"I want . . . you to do that . . . and

somehow I will . . . get you some . . . food."

"I have not thanked you for what you have brought me already," Vincent said. "I cannot remember ever having been so hungry before, not even in India."

"I will make . . . sure you are . . . never so hungry . . . again!" Charisa promised.

He smiled at her.

Then, as he moved into the shadows in the corner of the bed-room, she heard a slight sound as he opened the panelling.

He slipped through it, and a moment later the door closed and she was alone.

For a moment she could hardly believe it had all happened.

Vincent was home and he was able to hide in the secret passages where Gervais would not be able to find him.

She knew now why to be near Gervais had filled her with horror, why she had hated him not only for what he said and did but because of what he was.

Somehow, with God's help, Vincent would be restored to his rightful place.

Gervais would be driven away, back to Paris, from where he had come.

At the same time, she was aware he would not go easily.

If he had been unsuccessful in having Vincent murdered in India, perhaps he would find it easier to murder him here in England.

Then she was praying, praying fervently and desperately that while Gervais had failed three times to destroy Vincent, he would not have a chance to try again.

As soon as Charisa awoke in the morning she began to think of how she could provide food for Vincent without anyone being aware of it.

It was not going to be easy.

She would need to have her wits about her if she was not to arouse the suspicions of the people in the house.

Then Gervais would be aware that it might be easier to obtain food at breakfast-time than at any other time of the day.

When she went downstairs she carried with her a wickerwork basket in which she often put flowers.

As she had expected, her father was the only person having breakfast.

She kissed him good-morning and he said:

"As there appears to be no one about, I suggest you and I go riding. I have an appointment later on, so I have every excuse for not waiting for Gervais or anybody else."

"That would be lovely, Papa!" Charisa agreed.

The Colonel continued to eat his breakfast and at the same time read *The Times*.

The newspaper was propped up in front of him on a silver stand.

Thinking he would not be interested in her movements, Charisa went first to the sideboard.

There was the ham from which she had taken some slices last night.

There was brawn, which was a speciality of Mrs. Jones.

It had not yet been cut, and she took several slices.

When she had done so, she glanced back to see if her father was watching her.

He was opening the newspaper and she could not even see his face behind it.

Carefully, she transferred the pieces of brawn into her basket.

She covered them with a piece of paper she had put at the bottom.

She then added several slices of ham, and two pieces of toast.

Between them she put a large piece of butter.

By the time she had done this, her father had replaced *The Times* on its stand.

Charisa put the basket under the table at the place where she intended to sit.

She then collected her own breakfast from

the *entrée* dishes on the other sideboard.

She had nearly finished when, as had happened the day before, the *Comte* came into the room.

Before he could say good-morning, Charisa hurriedly got to her feet.

She picked up her basket and put it over her arm.

"I am late," the *Comte* said in a contrite voice, "but I cannot believe anyone so beautiful can be so hard-hearted as to leave the moment I arrive!"

"I have to get ready to take all the jumps in the field where we were yesterday," Charisa said. "I have challenged Papa to a contest."

She fled from the room as she spoke.

She hoped the *Comte* would not want to join them if it was a question of jumping.

Then she ran up the stairs and into her bedroom.

She was half-afraid the housemaids might be there making the bed.

But to her relief she saw that they had already done so.

She pressed the secret catch, opened the panel, and put the basket inside.

Shutting it again, she picked up her riding-hat and gloves.

She came down the stairs just as her

father was leaving the Breakfast-Room.

"Is the *Comte* joining us?" she asked in a whisper.

"Not if we hurry!" the Colonel replied.

His eyes were twinkling and she knew that he enjoyed out-witting the *Comte,* for whom he had no liking.

They hurried off to the stables.

It was with the greatest difficulty that Charisa refrained from telling her father what had happened last night.

She knew, however, that Vincent was right in thinking it would be dangerous.

Besides, as he said, he had no proof that Gervais had tried to murder him.

But there was nobody else who would benefit by his death.

Yet Charisa thought and thought about it.

But the more she thought, the more difficult it seemed to produce any evidence that would stand up in a Court of Law.

She could only pray, as she had told Vincent she would do, that somehow, by some miracle, they would find what they sought.

When she and her father returned to the house, the *Comte* and Gervais greeted them reproachfully.

"You knew I wanted to ride with you," Gervais said to Charisa.

"You will have to learn country ways,"

she replied lightly. "Papa and I always ride early, and besides, he has an appointment this morning."

Gervais looked questioningly at the Colonel.

"I hope you do not mind," the Colonel said, "but I have told my Race-Horse Manager to come here to see me, otherwise it would mean returning home."

"Of course I do not want you to go home," Gervais said, "so I am delighted for you to make any arrangements which will prevent you from leaving us."

"Thank you," the Colonel said.

"How many race-horses do you have?" Gervais enquired. "And are they successful?"

There was a note in his voice which told Charisa he was really asking if they made any money.

She turned away.

She was thinking how horrible it was that this craving for money should have made him commit murder.

Madame Dubus joined them a little later.

It was then Charisa realised they were all waiting for the party from Paris.

She learnt they were to arrive in time for luncheon.

"I made arrangements for my friends to stay in London last night," she heard

Gervais telling her father, "as it was too late for them to come here. They stayed at Claridge's, where I was quite sure they would be comfortable."

"Yes, of course," the Colonel agreed.

"I have sent carriages to meet them at the Station," Gervais went on, "and Mr. Sheldon assures me they will arrive here at twelve-thirty."

"It will be pleasant for you to have your friends around you," the Colonel said, "and perhaps it would be better for Charisa and me to return home."

It was with difficulty that Charisa prevented herself from giving a cry of horror.

She had forgotten that she had told her father she wished to go home as soon as possible.

But now Vincent was in the house and depending on her.

It was impossible for her to leave.

Before she could say anything, however, Gervais exclaimed:

"But how can you suggest anything so unkind? Of course I want you to stay, Colonel, and I am longing for Charisa to meet my friends. Please, do not even think of leaving me!"

"And I will not allow you to do so," *Madame* Dubus said in a caressing voice.

She looked up at the Colonel and slipped her arm through his.

"Do you not realise, *mon brave*," she asked, "that we all love you very much and enjoy more than it is possible to put into words having you with us?"

"That is exactly what I was going to say myself!" Gervais exclaimed.

There was nothing the Colonel could do but say he was very flattered by their kindness.

Of course, he added, he was looking forward to meeting the party from Paris.

They arrived in the carriages punctually at half-past-twelve.

When Charisa saw them, she realised they were just what she had expected.

First of all, the women appeared, and they were as smart and gushing as *Madame* Dubus.

At the same time, there was something about them which Charisa did not like.

She supposed it was because they were friends of Gervais.

She was sure too that her mother would not have approved of them.

The three men were very much like the *Comte*.

They were over-dressed, ingratiatingly complimentary, and had hard, bold eyes which somehow made her feel embarrassed.

The fourth man, she realised at once, was Gervais's Private Chaplain.

He was wearing a cassock.

When he took off his flat-brimmed clerical hat, she saw that the top of his head was bald and his hair at the sides was white.

As Gervais introduced him, she knew there was nothing spiritual about him.

She looked at his coarse-featured face, the darkness under his eyes, and the heavy lines at the sides of his lips.

It was strange, but he appeared somewhat debauched.

He certainly accepted freely the glasses of champagne that were being handed round.

Three times his glass was refilled before they went in to luncheon.

The conversation was, she supposed, witty.

But there were so many innuendos in all their conversation, she found it hard to follow.

Gervais's friends certainly seemed fond of him.

They listened with respect to what he had to say and appeared always to agree to anything he suggested.

The women, like *Madame* Dubus, flirted with the men, including her father.

The men paid her extravagant compliments. Charisa was conscious all the time, however, of an expression in their eyes that she did not like.

It was difficult to interpret what it meant, but she knew she shrank from looking at them.

Luncheon was as usual delicious, and she was wondering how to procure some food for Vincent.

There was certainly nothing she could take from the Dining-Room.

They went back into the Salon.

Charisa realised a large plate of *pâté* sandwiches which had been handed round with the champagne was practically untouched.

She looked at it, wondering how she could get it to Vincent, and had a sudden idea.

Picking up the plate, she walked towards the long windows.

"Where are you going, *Mademoiselle?*" one of the Frenchmen asked as she passed him.

"To feed the birds," Charisa replied. "I will not be a moment."

Before he could rise from his chair to accompany her, she slipped out through the window.

She ran along the side of the house and in through a garden-door.

As she ran up the stairs, she was sure that at this hour the staff would have finished and she would see no one.

She reached her own room, locked the door, and opened the panel.

There was no one there.

The basket in which she had left Vincent his breakfast was waiting for her and was empty.

She picked it up and was just about to put the *pâté* sandwiches into it when Vincent appeared.

He was looking very different from how he had looked last night.

Shaved, his hair brushed, and in his own clothes, he looked very handsome.

"How is my Guardian Angel this morning?" he asked. "And thank you for my breakfast."

"I am afraid you will have to make do with *pâté* sandwiches for luncheon," Charisa answered, "and I have to take the plate back."

"You are being wonderful," Vincent answered, "and you know how grateful I am."

He put the sandwiches into the basket and said:

"I do not much care for the look of those people who arrived to-day from Paris!"

"You saw them?" Charisa answered.

"I had a glimpse of them when they entered the hall, then I moved away."

"Why did you do that?"

"It was a mistake to stare at anyone in case they become instinctively aware of it," Vincent replied.

"Yes, of course, you are quite right!" Charisa agreed. "But I wanted you to see the awful little man whom Gervais describes as his 'Private Chaplain.' "

Vincent stared at her.

"Private Chaplain?" he questioned.

"I have not had time to tell you," Charisa said, "but the Vicar whom we all love — and I am sure you must remember —"

"Of course I do!" Vincent interrupted.

"He is very upset," Charisa went on, "because Gervais has told him he is not to hold the monthly Services in the Chapel because he has sent for his own Chaplain."

"I find that hard to believe," Vincent remarked, "and I shall certainly have a look at this man."

He was frowning, and Charisa said quickly:

"I must take the plate and go back. I told the Frenchman — whose name I cannot remember — that I was taking the *pâté* sandwiches to feed the birds."

Vincent laughed.

"Whatever you call me, I am very grateful! Thank you, Charisa!"

She shut the panel door and hurried down the stairs and back into the garden.

As she sauntered casually back into the Salon, she realised the party were all talking in French, and they were laughing uproariously at some joke.

From the expression on her father's face, she was sure it was somewhat *risqué*.

As she put the plate down on the table, Gervais rose from where he was sitting.

Walking towards her, he put his arm round her waist.

"I want you to look at my lovely young cousin," he said to his friends.

Because he was touching her, Charisa felt once again the revulsion she had felt before.

This time, knowing he was a murderer, it was now even more intense.

She would have moved away, but he would not let her go.

"Have you ever seen anyone so beautiful, so innocent, or so pure?" Gervais asked.

He was speaking in French so that it did not sound quite as crude as it would have done in English.

At the same time, Charisa felt embarrassed.

"How could anyone not worship such beauty?" Gervais went on. "And that is why I know you will think I am a very lucky man

150

to have such an adorable and lovely — relative."

There was a pause before he said the last word.

Charisa knew that what he wanted to say was *"fiancée."*

Determinedly, she moved away from him and went towards her father.

She was not certain he had heard what Gervais was saying because *Madame* Dubus was whispering something in his ear.

She stood in front of him, then put out her hand to take his.

"I have something very important to talk to you about, Papa," she said. "Please . . . come with me."

Her father looked surprised, but he rose to his feet.

She slipped her arm through his and drew him towards the door.

Only when they were outside did she say:

"I am sorry, Papa, to take you away, but Gervais was talking about me to his friends in a vulgar manner, which made me feel uneasy and I had to get away."

"I understand," the Colonel said, "and I think Gervais had too much to drink at luncheon. It is best to take no notice of him."

"That is what I wanted to do," Charisa said.

"I suppose, if we were sensible, we would go home now," the Colonel remarked.

Charisa was silent.

She was wondering whether it would be possible to persuade Vincent to go with them.

Then she knew it was impossible.

The only chance he had of finding anything against Gervais was to be on the spot, to stay in the house without anybody being aware of it.

With an effort she said in a very different tone:

"No, of course not, Papa. I am being foolish, though, quite frankly, I find all these extravagant compliments embarrassing."

"Of course you do," the Colonel argued.

He put his arm around his daughter's shoulders and pulled her against him.

"We will stay for another twenty-four hours," he said, "and after that, whatever Gervais may say, we are going home."

Charisa did not answer.

She was only praying that twenty-four hours would be enough for Vincent to find the evidence he wanted.

Then it would be Gervais who would be leaving the Priory, and not they.

chapter six

Charisa rose earlier than usual.

When she went into the Breakfast-Room there was nobody there.

The servants did not wait at breakfast.

She knew, therefore, she had the room to herself until her father appeared.

She quickly filled her basket with even more of the cold dishes than she had done yesterday.

She had just put two rosy peaches into the basket and slipped it under the table as she had the day before when her father came in.

"Good-morning, my dearest!" he said. "We are the first, as usual, and I suggest we go riding again before anyone in the party joins us."

Charisa was aware as he spoke that he had taken a dislike to Gervais's French guests.

She had thought at dinner that he was looking at them disapprovingly.

Despite the blandishments of *Madame* Dubus, he was uncomfortable.

Charisa thought he would insist on going home.

But when they did so, what would happen to Vincent?

'He must have found out something by now!' she thought.

She hurried over her breakfast.

Then she went upstairs, ostensibly to fetch her riding-hat and gloves.

She opened the panel in her bed-room and put the basket inside.

She had hoped that Vincent would be waiting for her.

There was, however, no sign of him.

There was nothing, therefore, she could do but go downstairs to where her father was waiting for her.

They had a delightful ride.

The horse on which Charisa was mounted took the jumps better than she had ever taken them before.

As her father had no engagements, they did not return to the Priory until it was growing late in the morning.

"I should think everyone is up by this time," Charisa said as they rode up to the front-door.

"I should hope so," her father said somewhat stiffly. "It is ridiculous for young men to rise so late when they are in the country!"

He spoke in his "Regimental Voice," and Charisa laughed.

Then she went upstairs to change from her riding-habit into a pretty, thin gown.

" 'Tis goin' t' be hot to-day," Bessy said as she helped her dress.

"I like the heat," Charisa answered, "but I will take a sunshade when I go out into the garden."

"You do that, Miss," Bessy said, "it'd be a crime to spoil your lovely skin."

Charisa smiled at her and went downstairs.

As she did so, she wondered if, as there appeared to be no one about, *pâté* sandwiches had been put again in the Sitting-Room.

She knew there would be champagne for the guests before luncheon.

She might be unable to get Vincent anything else at luncheon.

So she decided to take a few sandwiches now, and later in the day try to find him something for dinner.

She reached the door of what was known as the "Reynolds Room."

It had several portraits by that famous Artist on the walls.

She was just about to open the door when she thought that if Gervais were there alone, she had no wish to join him.

She turned the handle very cautiously so that she could slip away if he were there.

As she did so, she heard him say:

"We will have the Service to-night, and after that Charisa will have to marry me."

Charisa stiffened and stood still.

"Of course she will!" she heard *Madame* Dubus say. "Nobody else would offer for her!"

They both laughed.

Very quietly Charisa closed the door.

Then, because she was frightened, she ran upstairs.

What did Gervais mean by saying she would have to marry him?

Why would no one else wish to propose to her?

She could not imagine what he and *Madame* Dubus meant.

At the same time, she could feel her fear of them seeping through her breasts.

She reached her bed-room.

Running in, she shut the door and locked it behind her.

Then she opened the panel.

If Vincent was not there, she would have to find him.

However, to her relief he was standing just inside.

The basket she had left for him after breakfast was in his hand.

"Oh, Vincent," she exclaimed, "I am . . . f-frightened!"

"Frightened? Why? What has happened?" he asked.

"I . . . I went downstairs . . . and thought . . . I would . . . get you some . . . *pâté* sandwiches . . . from the . . . 'Reynolds Room.' "

She was speaking so breathlessly that Vincent stepped through the panel and put down the basket.

"What upset you there?" he asked.

"I heard . . . Gervais and . . . *Madame* Dubus . . . talking."

"Tell me what they said."

Charisa repeated their words.

Because they frightened her even more than they had already, she put out her hand to hold on to him.

His fingers closed over hers.

Then, as she finished repeating what *Madame* Dubus had said, he asked sharply:

"What did you say was the name of the woman with Gervais?"

"*Madame* Dubus. Ariste Dubus. She came . . . here with . . . Gervais. I thought . . . you must have . . . seen her."

"I saw her," Vincent replied, "but I did not know her name!"

He spoke in such a grim manner that Charisa looked at him questioningly before she said:

"What . . . does it . . . mean? What . . . are

they . . . planning? Why did Gervais . . . say that . . . after the Service . . . I would have . . . to marry . . . him?"

For a moment Vincent did not reply.

Then he asked:

"Where is your father?"

Charisa looked at him in surprise.

"He came upstairs to change . . . when I did. He will be in . . . his room."

"Fetch him!" Vincent said. "Fetch him quickly!"

"B-but you said . . . I was not . . . to tell," Charisa began.

"Do as I say!" Vincent said in an authoritative tone. "Bring your father here as quickly as you can!"

Charisa wanted him to explain why he had changed his mind.

But she thought, if she did not do as he asked immediately, her father might go downstairs.

She unlocked her bed-room door and ran down the corridor.

Her father's room was only a little way from her own.

When she reached it, she saw with relief that he was still there.

So was his Valet.

"I want to speak to . . . you, Papa," she said. "It is . . . important."

Wilkins tactfully withdrew.

The moment they were alone, Charisa went up to her father and put her hand on his arm.

"I want you to . . . come with . . . me, Papa, and try . . . not to be very . . . surprised at . . . what you . . . see."

"What are you talking about?" the Colonel asked. "Has that swine been upsetting you again?"

"No . . . no . . . it is not . . . Gervais," Charisa answered. "But please . . . come to . . . my room!"

The Colonel picked up his gold watch that was lying on the dressing-table.

He put it in the pocket of his waist-coat. Then he said:

"You are being very mysterious, my dear, but of course I will do anything you want."

Charisa slipped her hand into his.

Hurriedly, they walked down the passage to her room.

She opened the door, and the Colonel followed her in.

She was not surprised to see that Vincent was not there.

She knew he was hiding in case he should be seen by one of the housemaids.

Charisa shut the door and her father started to say:

"Now, what is all this about . . . ?"

The panel opened as he was speaking, and Vincent appeared.

For a moment the Colonel just stared at him, speechless.

Then he exclaimed:

"Vincent, my dear boy! You are alive? Why did you not let us know?"

"I have a lot to tell you, Colonel," Vincent said, "but no one knows I am here except Charisa."

"I do not understand," the Colonel said. "We were told you were dead!"

"I know," Vincent said grimly, "and it is only by a miracle, or rather three miracles, that I am alive to tell you what happened."

The Colonel was just about to say something, when Vincent turned towards Charisa.

"I want you to go downstairs, Charisa," he said, "and behave as if nothing has happened. In fact, make yourself very pleasant to everybody, including Gervais."

Charisa made a little grimace, and he said:

"I know, but your father and I are going to deal with everything, and later we will tell you what we have planned."

Charisa wanted to beg him to let her stay. But she thought it might prove dangerous, and she must therefore do as she was told.

"I will . . . go downstairs," she said a little reluctantly, "but . . . promise me . . . you will . . . tell me what . . . you and Papa are . . . planning to do."

"If I cannot tell you before," Vincent said, "go up to your room and lie down at about five o'clock. Say you have a headache and do not wish to be disturbed."

"I will do . . . that," Charisa said.

She touched her father's arm affectionately before she moved towards the door.

"It is wonderful to have Vincent back, Papa!" she said in a low voice.

Then she went out into the corridor.

She heard Vincent lock the door behind her.

She wished she could stay to hear what they were saying.

It was agonising to have to go downstairs, to be with all Gervais's French guests when she thought that something positive was happening at last.

It puzzled her what Gervais had meant by saying she would have to marry him after the Service.

It seemed very strange that they should have a Service on a Friday night.

Perhaps since his Private Chaplain had

arrived from Paris, Gervais thought he should hold one.

'I wish I could hide somewhere behind the panelling and hear what Vincent and Papa are saying,' she thought.

Resolutely, because she knew that she must obey Vincent's orders, she went into the "Reynolds Room."

The house-party was, as usual, drinking.

Their glasses were replenished as soon as they were empty.

It was nearly time for luncheon.

Charisa was expecting it to be announced, when her father came into the room.

She thought he deliberately did not look at her.

He walked to where Gervais was sitting with a glass of champagne in his hand.

"I hope you will allow me, Gervais," he said, "to order my carriage, as I have to go home immediately."

"What has happened, Colonel?" Gervais enquired.

"I have just been informed that there has been an accident involving one of my staff, who has been injured."

He paused to say insistently:

"You will understand that I must see that the Doctor is summoned, and find out if the injury is really serious."

"Yes, of course," Gervais agreed, "but surely you can wait until after luncheon?"

"It is very kind of you, but I will have something to eat at home," the Colonel replied.

"Well, I hope it is not too serious," Gervais said, "and of course you will come back as quickly as you can. We will look after Charisa in the meantime."

"I am sure you will," the Colonel answered.

He walked across the room to Charisa and said:

"Do not worry, my dear. It is old Eliza, who was never steady on her feet!"

He pressed her fingers as he spoke and Charisa exclaimed:

"Oh, I am sorry, Papa, but I am sure Dr. White will look after her."

"Of course he will," the Colonel said, "and I will not be any longer than I can help."

He kissed her cheek.

She knew by the pressure of his hand that he was approving the attitude she had taken.

Yet, as he went from the room, she longed to go with him.

She realised why he was taking his carriage.

If he had been going home alone, he would have ridden.

That he was taking his carriage meant he was taking Vincent with him.

But where were they going, and why?

It was difficult, because she was thinking of them, to listen to the compliments she was being paid, or to respond to the witty remarks the Frenchmen on either side of her at luncheon were making.

Because she was so anxious, she had no idea what she ate or drank.

She found herself continually glancing across the table at the Chaplain.

He appeared to be drinking more than usual and looked, she thought, very unpleasant.

It seemed extraordinary that Gervais could not have found a more attractive-looking man.

When luncheon was over, Gervais offered to take them driving on a tour of the Estate.

As they had all had a lot to drink, they agreed to his suggestion somewhat half-heartedly.

Finally, with the exception of the Ladies and the Chaplain, they set off in three different vehicles.

The Frenchman offered to race Gervais, but he declined.

"I want you to admire my possessions," he said, "and just be careful of how you treat my horses!"

"How he enjoys being a rich man!" the *Comte* said to another man.

He spoke in a low voice so that Gervais did not hear him.

As she walked away she was praying that Gervais's enjoyment would not last long.

She, of course, had to drive with him.

Fortunately, because the Chaise was fairly large, there was room for the *Comte* also.

She, however, felt squeezed between two men.

Because such proximity to them made her feel almost physically sick, she said very little.

All she could think of was that Vincent and her father were planning some way by which Gervais could be brought to justice.

She had no idea what it could be.

'With Vincent in his rightful place as the Marquis of Mawdelyn, everything will be so different,' she thought.

She knew she would have enjoyed every moment of driving with Vincent round the estate.

Gervais was interested only in what was bringing in money.

It was money she was sure would not be expended on the Priory, and certainly not in doing anything for those he employed.

He swept past the men working in the fields without raising his hat to them as Vincent would have done.

When they stopped at a farm, she thought he was aggressive in the way he spoke to the Farmer.

He ignored the man's wife, even though she curtsied respectfully to him.

"I hate him! I hate him!" Charisa was saying over and over again as they drove home.

"You are very silent, Charisa!" Gervais said unexpectedly.

"I am a little tired," Charisa replied. "I think when we get back I will lie down before dinner."

"That is a very good idea," Gervais agreed, "because tonight I want you to look even more beautiful that you have ever looked before."

"Why tonight especially?" Charisa asked.

"I will give you the answer to that later," Gervais replied.

"You always look beautiful!" the *Comte* said in a caressing voice. "In fact, if you can look more lovely than you do at this moment, I shall find it hard to believe you are human!"

"At the moment I feel very human!" Charisa said. "I think it must be the sun that has given me a headache."

"Then go and lie down as soon as we get in," Gervais said, "and before dinner I will send you up a special drink which will make you feel like dancing among the stars!"

Before Charisa could speak, the *Comte* laughed.

"You are being poetical, Gervais!"

"I have every reason to be," Gervais replied, "because I am looking forward to this evening."

"So am I," the *Comte* said, "in fact more than I can say in words."

"What is happening this evening?" Charisa asked.

"Something very important," Gervais said, "and that is why you must look beautiful."

They arrived back at the Priory as he spoke, and he pulled in the horses.

As Charisa got out, she was aware that Gervais and the *Comte* were exchanging glances as if they were sharing some secret joke.

Because she was frightened by what they were saying, she ran up the stairs.

She felt as if she were enveloped by something dangerous.

When she reached her bed-room it was a relief to find that Bessy was already there.

"I have a headache, Bessy," she said, "and I am going to lie down until it is time for dinner."

"Now, that's sensible!" Bessy exclaimed. "I says you'd find th' sun too much for you to-day."

She undid Charisa's gown at the back.

When she had put on a pretty, lace-trimmed nightgown, Charisa got into bed.

Bessy lowered the blinds a little and said as she left the room:

"I'll see you're not disturbed, Miss Charisa, an'd you 'ave a bit of 'shut-eye.' It'll do you good!"

As soon as she had gone, Charisa got out of bed and locked the door.

Then she opened the panel, hoping she would find Vincent waiting inside.

There was, however, no sign of him.

Disappointed, she got back into bed feeling more frightened than ever.

It was, in fact, nearly an hour later before the panel opened and he came into the room.

Charisa gave a cry of delight and sat up in bed.

"Vincent!" she exclaimed. "I thought . . . you had . . . forgotten me!"

168

He came towards her and sat down, as he had done before, on the side of the bed.

Then he took her hand in his and said:

"I have been thinking about you every moment since I left here."

"And I have . . . been thinking . . . of you!" Charisa answered.

She looked up at him and felt his fingers tighten on hers.

In that moment she knew she loved him.

She had always loved him, she thought, even when she was a child.

But she had not realised it until this moment.

She felt as if it were a revelation that came to her from Heaven.

For a moment they just looked at each other.

Then Vincent said:

"You have been very brave and wonderful. Now I am going to ask you to be even braver than you have been already."

"Why?" Charisa asked. "What have you and Papa been planning."

"Ever since I came back," Vincent said in a low voice, "you know I have been trying to find some way by which I could claim my rightful position as the Head of the Family without being murdered by Gervais."

"I know that," Charisa said, "and I have

. . . been desperately, terribly afraid of what . . . he would do if . . . he knew you were . . . here."

"It was you who told me to-day what we could do," Vincent replied, "but it is not going to be easy."

"Tell . . . me what it is . . . tell me quickly!" Charisa begged.

"You heard Gervais saying that there was to be a Service held here to-night," Vincent said. "That 'Service,' Charisa, will be a Black Mass!"

Charisa stared at him in astonishment.

For a moment she could not remember what a Black Mass was.

Then, as she did remember, she gave a cry of horror.

"You mean . . . you cannot mean . . . !"

"Gervais is a Satanist!" Vincent answered. "I blame myself for not remembering that one of my friends hinted at it a long time ago after he had been to Paris."

"A . . . Satanist!" Charisa exclaimed beneath her breath.

"You gave me the clue," Vincent explained, "when you told me that the woman he brought here was *Madame* Ariste Dubus. She is the sister of one of the most notorious Satanists in Paris, who uses drugs which induce hallucinations!"

"And . . . you think . . . that she . . . does the . . . same," Charisa whispered.

"I imagine all those people downstairs who have come here as Gervais's friends worship Satan, just as he does. And that is why they are having a Service to-night."

Charisa made a little murmur of horror, and Vincent said gently:

"You realise they intend to use you in that Service?"

Charisa's eyes widened.

"I . . . I do not . . . believe I . . ." she began.

Then, almost as the words left her lips, she added:

"Save me . . . save . . . me!"

Vaguely at the back of her mind she remembered that the Black Mass was said over the naked body of a Virgin.

She had heard that strange orgies took place later.

Now she understood why Gervais had said she would have to marry him afterwards, why *Madame* Dubus had said nobody else would want her.

"Save . . . me!" she begged again.

Now she was clinging on to Vincent with both hands.

"You know I will do that," he said in his deep voice, "and your father and I have been to see the Chief Constable, General

Sir Henry Barker."

"Then . . . you will . . . have Gervais . . . arrested!"

She spoke frantically.

She was still clinging to Vincent as if she were afraid he might go away and leave her to her fate.

Unexpectedly, he turned round so that he was sitting with his back against the pillows.

He put his arms round Charisa and held her close against him.

She put her head on his shoulder.

"Now listen, my darling," he said.

Charisa was so surprised at the endearment that for the moment she forgot her terror and looked up at him.

He smiled as he said:

"I love you! I have loved you ever since I came back home and you were so unutterably brave."

He pulled her a little closer before he said:

"No, that is not true! I loved you before I went away, but I thought my love was for a child. When I saw you again, I knew that you were the only person who has ever really mattered to me in my life!"

"Oh . . . Vincent . . . is that . . . true?"

"I will make you believe it, my Precious One, but for the moment we must concentrate on freeing ourselves from this terrible evil which threatens you."

"As it threatens you," Charisa added.

"With God's help we shall both survive," Vincent said. "But I am afraid, my precious little love, that you have to do something extremely unpleasant before Gervais can be arrested."

For a moment, because his tone was so serious, Charisa trembled.

Then she said:

"If it will save you, I will do . . . anything . . . anything you ask of me."

"I knew that was what you would say," Vincent said as he smiled. "Could anybody be more wonderful!"

She felt his lips against her forehead.

Then, as if he forced himself to go on, he began:

"Your father and I drove from here to see the Chief Constable . . ."

"How did you manage to get away with Papa?" Charisa interrupted.

"I slipped out through the garden-door," Vincent explained, "and went down through the bushes to the end of the Park. No one saw me go into the carriage. Your father was driving alone but the hood was up."

"That was sensible of Papa!" Charisa exclaimed.

"We saw no one who might have recognised me before we reached the house of the Chief Constable. As you can imagine, the General was astonished to see me."

"But I am sure he was very glad! He was always very fond of Uncle George."

"He was delighted," Vincent replied, "especially because he knew a lot about Gervais's activities in Paris."

"You mean . . . he knew . . . he was a . . . Satanist?"

"He had heard rumours that he was dabbling in Black Magic, which is very prevalent in France at the moment, and he is sure that the man whom Gervais refers to as his Private Chaplain is an unfrocked Priest."

Charisa made a little murmur of disgust, but she did not interrupt.

Vincent went on:

"The Chief Constable agreed with your father that all these people must be expelled from our country, and Gervais can be arrested under the laws regarding Witchcraft."

Charisa was about to give a sigh of relief when he added:

"But, of course, he has to have proof of it!"

There was silence.

Then Charisa asked in a small voice that

Vincent could hardly hear:

"Do you . . . need me to . . . take part . . . in the . . . Service?"

"That is what they are hoping you will agree to do, and that, my precious, is what I am asking you to do."

"How . . . how can . . . I?"

Vincent held her so tightly that she could hardly breathe.

"I swear to you that no one will touch you, except to carry you into the Chapel," he promised. "The Chief Constable, your father, and I have planned that we will interrupt the Service before they actually touch you. Then Gervais will be arrested, as will all those present."

His voice was very tender as he said:

"I know it is a great deal to ask of you, but you must believe that God will protect you, and so will I."

His voice sharpened as he added:

"I will kill Gervais myself rather than let him touch you! At the same time, my darling, there is nothing we can do unless we have the proof that he is actually holding a Black Mass."

"And . . . what you are . . . saying is that he . . . cannot do it . . . without me!"

"That is true," Vincent said, "for it might take them a long time to find another Virgin for the ceremony. In the meantime, Gervais will do everything possible to try to marry you."

There was silence. Then Charisa said:

"T-tell me what I . . . have to do."

"You have a choice," Vincent said. "Before the Satanists perform a Black Mass, they have a huge dinner at which they eat and drink in abundance. This, of course, is to prove themselves different from the Christians, who fast before receiving the Sacrament."

"Do I have to be . . . at the dinner?"

"Not if you allow them to render you unconscious before it starts," Vincent replied.

"That is . . . what they . . . mean to . . . do," Charisa whispered. "Gervais said when I was . . . driving with . . . him that he would . . . send up a . . . special drink to my bedroom to make me . . . feel well for this . . . evening because it is a very . . . important . . . occasion."

"If you drink what he sends you," Vincent said, " you will be unaware of anything that happens afterwards. It is, in fact, a merciful action on the part of the Satanists rather than submit their victim, fully conscious, to the appalling horrors which happen at the end of the Service."

"What . . . is the . . . alternative?" Charisa questioned.

"It is that you pretend to be unconscious, which means that just the same you will not have to dine with the party."

He paused before he went on:

"Afterwards they will carry you to the Chapel and lay you on the altar, thinking you have no idea of what is happening."

Charisa did not speak, and he said very quietly:

"It is entirely up to you, my darling. You must do what you wish."

"I think I . . . would rather . . . know what is . . . happening, and especially be . . . aware of the . . . moment when . . . you save . . . me," Charisa said.

"You are quite sure?" Vincent asked.

"It is more . . . frightening to be . . . unconscious and not to . . . know when I . . . shall wake . . . up."

"Very well," he said. "But somehow you must be clever enough to make them believe you have drunk the drugged wine."

"I . . . I am sure . . . I can do . . . that," Charisa said, "but you . . . promise me you will . . . not be far . . . away?"

"I shall be on the other side of the panel just in case something goes wrong before they leave you to go downstairs and gorge themselves," Vincent said.

He smiled at her re-assuringly before he continued:

"After that, when they carry you to the Chapel, remember it will only be a few minutes before your father and I, with the help of the Police, will save you."

chapter seven

Vincent sat with Charisa for a long time.

He kissed her, comforted her, and re-assured her.

Finally he glanced at the clock by her bed and said:

"I think, my darling, I must leave you now. You must unlock your door, otherwise people will think it strange that you have barred yourself in."

"Yes . . . of course," Charisa said in a trembling voice.

"I know you are frightened," Vincent said, "but I swear to you that once this is over, we will never think of it again. We will make the Priory a happy place, where there is only love, starting with you and me."

He kissed her as he spoke.

Charisa knew that the love he was giving her was the perfect, sacred love in which she had always believed.

It was the love which came from God, and nothing evil or cruel could destroy it.

At the same time, when Vincent rose to leave her she was trembling.

"You . . . will be . . . near me?" she asked.

"I will be near you," he answered, "thinking about you, praying for you, and loving you."

The way he spoke was so moving that she felt the tears come into her eyes.

Then, with a last kiss, he walked across the room.

He unlocked the door so that she would not have to get out of bed.

He smiled at her re-assuringly before he disappeared through the secret panel.

She shut her eyes, praying that everything would go right, that Gervais and his evil Satanists would be defeated.

When they all went back to France she need never think of them again.

She knew that the Vicar would bless the Chapel and take away the evil they had left behind them.

She understood now why Gervais had re-moved the Cross and the ancient candlesticks.

She wondered what he intended to put in their place.

Then she remembered reading that for a Black Mass they had on the altar a Crucifix upside-down.

The thought made her tremble again.

For a moment she wanted to run to the panel and tell Vincent she could not go ahead with it.

Then she remembered that she was saving him, saving him so that he could take his rightful place as the Marquis of Mawdelyn.

"I would do . . . anything . . . anything in the . . . world to . . . save . . . Vincent," she told herself.

She was not alone for long, for Bessy soon came in to say:

"I'm bringing in your bath, Miss Charisa, then I'll get your gown ready."

She was followed into the room as she spoke by two housemaids.

They were carrying a bath, which they set down in front of the fire-place.

It was, of course, too hot for there to be any need for a fire.

Next they brought in two large brass cans, one containing hot water the other cold.

Charisa knew that a footman would have carried them upstairs, as they were too heavy for a woman.

Bessy scented the bath with oil of violets.

The flowers were distilled every year at the Priory ever since Charisa could remember.

It was her mother who had asked for violets when previously they had always used heliotrope.

The soft sweet scent reminded Charisa of her mother.

As she washed herself she prayed that her mother would be near her in the ordeal which lay ahead.

She had just finished drying herself with a large towel when there was a knock on the door.

Bessy went to see who it was.

Then she stood back to allow *Madame* Dubus to come into the room.

"I came to see how you are feeling, *ma petite*," she said in her usual gushing manner. "Your Cousin Gervais, who is always thinking of you, has sent this delicious drink which will sweep away your headache and make you enjoy the very special evening we have ahead of us."

Still wrapped in the towel, Charisa asked:

"Do tell me what is being . . . planned."

"I will in a moment," *Madame* Dubus said, "but I think your maid wants to remove your bath."

As she spoke she looked at Bessy, who hurriedly called in the two housemaids.

They carried the bath and the cans out of the bed-room.

As they did so, Charisa had an idea.

She rose and opened a drawer of the Chest of Drawers.

It was where she had put her jewel-case which she had brought with her from home.

It was a large leather case which had belonged to her mother and much of her mother's jewellery was in it.

Not the tiara or the huge necklace she had worn on special occasions.

Nor the rings which her husband had given her on every anniversary.

Instead, there was a small necklace of pearls and brooches which were not too overwhelmingly grand for a young girl.

There was also a collection of charm bracelets, pendants, and jewelled clips for the hair.

As soon as Bessy had gone, *Madame* Dubus picked up the glass she had put down on the side-table.

She carried it across the room to Charisa, who had deliberately chosen to sit on the side of her bed.

She had no wish for *Madame* Dubus to touch her more than was necessary.

"Now drink this," *Madame* Dubus said. "You will really enjoy it, and I know you will feel when you have taken it as if you are flying up into the sky."

Charisa remembered what Gervais had said about "dancing amongst the stars." She knew the drink must contain a powerful drug.

She took the glass in her hand and said:

"It is so kind of Gervais to think of me,

and while I am drinking it, will you be kind enough to choose what jewellery you think I should wear to-night? It is in that drawer."

She pointed as she spoke to the Chest of Drawers.

She knew that while *Madame* Dubus was looking at her jewellery she would have her back to her.

"I am delighted to do that," *Madame* Dubus said, "and to-night you must look like a Fairy Princess."

Charisa laughed.

"I think that is unlikely, but perhaps I had better wear some of my mother's diamonds."

As if she found the idea of looking for them irresistible, *Madame* Dubus walked across the room.

As soon as she did so, Charisa tipped the contents of the glass onto the carpet between the bed and the bedside table.

There was no possibility of anybody noticing it there unless they were brushing the carpet.

Holding the empty glass as if her hand suddenly felt limp, Charisa said in a faltering voice:

"I . . . I feel . . . strange . . . I . . . I think I am . . . going . . . to . . ."

Her voice trailed away and she fell backwards onto the bed.

"*Tiens!*" *Madame* Dubus exclaimed.

She turned round and hurried back. Charisa could not see her, but she felt sure she was looking at her with satisfaction.

Then she lifted her legs up onto the bed.

Taking away the towel with which she had dried herself, *Madame* pulled over her one of the satin and lace bed-covers.

She stood for a moment looking down at Charisa before she picked up the glass that had rolled onto the floor.

Then she walked towards the door.

She opened it, and as she did so she must have found Bessy standing just outside.

Charisa heard her say:

"Your mistress is not feeling well and has gone back to sleep. No one is to disturb her — no one — do you understand? You are not to go in and wake her up, but let her sleep."

"D'you mean Miss Charisa ain't goin' down to dinner?" Bessy asked in astonishment.

"I mean exactly that," *Madame* Dubus replied. "If you wake her up, His Lordship will be very angry!"

"I'll leave 'er alone, Ma'am," Bessy said, "but it seems strange t'me!"

"You are here to obey orders," *Madame*

Dubus said aggressively, "and if you do not do as you are told, you will be sent away without a reference."

Charisa could imagine Bessy's consternation at being spoken to in such a manner.

Then, as if *Madame* Dubus thought she could not trust her, she said:

"To make sure you do not interfere, I am going to lock the door."

As she spoke, she took the key from inside the room and put it in the lock on the other side.

She pulled the door to, and Charisa heard the key turn in the lock.

When it did so, she sat up, and was acutely aware that she was naked.

She pulled the satin cover over her breasts, and as she did so Vincent opened the panel.

Charisa would have cried out in her delight at seeing him, but he put his finger to his lips.

He quietly came across to the bed.

Only when he was very close did he say in a whisper:

"You were marvellous, my precious!"

"You heard what she said?"

"I heard everything," he answered. "I cannot imagine how I could have been so lucky as to have found anyone as won-

186

derful and clever as you."

He put his arms around her and was conscious as he did so that her back was bare.

He kissed her very gently.

Then, as Charisa smiled, he laid her back against the pillows.

"I have to leave you now, my little love," he said, "because your father may want to have a last word with me before he attends that revolting dinner at which they are going to gorge themselves."

"Does Papa have to go to it?" Charisa asked.

"He is not certain. He thinks he may be offered the same drink they tried to give you," Vincent replied. "In fact, I shall be surprised if that does not happen."

"But he . . . will not . . . drink it?"

"Of course not," Vincent said as he smiled.

He kissed her very gently before he said:

"Leave everything to me, and just remember that after to-night we shall be free to love each other and be married."

Charisa's eyes lit up.

"You . . . really and . . . truly want . . . me to be your . . . wife?"

"I will tell you how much I want you and how much I love you as soon as this nightmare is over."

He moved away from her as he spoke. She had no idea how much he wanted to stay and how much even at this crucial moment she excited him.

He had never imagined anyone could look so lovely as she did.

Her hair was falling over her shoulders and her hands with their long fingers held the satin cover over her breasts.

As he reached the panel he smiled and looked at her for a long moment.

She could see the love in his eyes.

For a moment she forgot everything else but the fact that Vincent loved her as she loved him.

It was almost too poignant to believe that they could be together, that once they were married, nothing could ever hurt them again.

Then she was afraid she was asking too much.

She began to pray frantically that God would make it all happen.

"Please . . . God . . . please . . ." she was saying over and over again.

Moving along the secret passage, Vincent peeped into the room where the Colonel was changing for dinner.

He was not surprised to see that he was

lying apparently unconscious on the bed in his evening-clothes.

There was no sign of his Valet.

Vincent knew the Colonel would have told Wilkins to leave him and not to come back before he had supposedly drunk the drugged wine.

'Gervais has certainly set the stage for his unspeakable crime!' Vincent thought.

He moved on down a secret passage which enabled him to look into the Mawdelyn Chapel.

As he had expected, Gervais and his friends had been busy preparing for the Black Mass.

Upside-down on the altar was a large Crucifix which must have come with the Chaplain from Paris.

There were six long black candles.

They were stuck into small skulls which he did not want to think were the size of very small children.

A cloth embroidered with several occult signs had been put on the altar. It was obviously where they intended to lay Charisa.

On the side-table there was a loaf of bread, a knife, a chalice, and a decanter of wine.

Vincent was sure it contained drugs which would inflame those who drank it.

Just as he suspected, all the Satanists had already been taking drugs before they attended the Service.

He looked through the secret spy-hole for only a few seconds before he moved away.

He was sickened at the thought of what would take place.

Now all he could do was to wait until the Colonel joined him.

It seemed to Charisa a very long time elapsed before she heard the key turning in the lock.

She closed her eyes knowing that her arms were lying limply under the bed-cover.

She heard several people come into the room.

Then *Madame* Dubus said in a thick, rather unsteady voice:

"Pick her up carefully, *mes braves!* We do not want any accidents!"

She was speaking in French.

The man who answered her, Charisa thought, was the *Comte*.

"No, of course not! We will be very careful with anything so precious."

He too sounded as if he had been drinking.

As she felt his hands under her bare shoulders, Charisa wanted to scream.

She was aware as another man lifted her feet that they left the bed-cover over her body.

They moved towards the door.

Madame Dubus gave instructions as they did so, and they proceeded down the main staircase.

Charisa wondered what had happened to the footmen who were usually in attendance.

As there was no sound from them, she guessed that Gervais had given orders that they were to remain in their own quarters.

It was growing quite late by now because they had taken a long time over dinner.

Then suddenly Charisa was aware of voices chanting.

She knew the sound came from the Chapel.

She could not understand the words, and the sound made her shrink within herself.

She was desperately afraid.

The voices grew louder and louder.

Now she knew that those who were carrying her had entered the Chapel.

There was a strong smell of incense.

As the voices rose higher and louder, she realised that they were chanting some sort of prayer.

They were not speaking in French or in English, but in Latin.

As she was carried up the short aisle she could recognise several names.

Nisroch, the god of Hatred, Moloch, the fatalist who devoured children, and Adramelech, the god of Murder.

She had read their names years ago in a book on Witchcraft.

Now the voices of Gervais's guests cried out in French:

"Beelzebub, Adramelech, Lucifer, come to us! Master of Darkness, we implore thee! Satan, we are thy slaves! Come! Come! Illuminate us with thy presence!"

Charisa realised by this time she was lying on the altar.

The odour of incense was overpowering.

Then a man, and she knew it was the Chaplain, began a prayer in Latin.

He was saying the words backwards.

She was thankful that they had not yet removed the bed-cover from her body.

She was trembling and was afraid they might realise she was not unconscious, as she was supposed to be.

The first prayer was followed by another.

Now the congregation, if that was the right word for those present, joined in.

Charisa realised they were once again

calling up Satan into their midst and invoking devils.

"Belilah in eternal revolt and now anarchy — Ashtaroth, Nehamah, Astarte in debauchery."

It was then she became desperately afraid that the evil which she could feel emanating all around would somehow affect her.

She began to pray to herself.

The words of the evening Collect she had learnt as a small child came to her.

"Lighten our darkness, we beseech Thee, O Lord, and by Thy great mercy defend us from all perils and dangers of this night, for the love of Thy only Son, our Saviour, Jesus Christ."

She said it once.

Then as the horror of what was happening swept over her she began it again.

"Lighten our darkness . . ."

It was then a voice rang out from the back of the Chapel.

"Stop this blasphemy!"

It was the voice of her father, strong and commanding, as he would have spoken as a soldier in the face of the enemy.

Immediately there was silence.

Now Charisa knew that her father and Vincent were marching up the aisle side by side.

It was then that the Chaplain gave a cry of horror.

Even as he did so, Gervais pushed him to one side.

Charisa could not help opening her eyes to see what was happening.

Gervais was wearing a vestment embroidered with mysterious signs.

The garment was open down the front, and beneath it he was naked.

He was now towering over her.

Before he spoke she saw the sharp-pointed knife in his right hand which he had taken from the table.

With his left he swept the cloth from her body, leaving her naked as he said:

"Come one step nearer and I will kill this woman, piercing her through the heart!"

He spoke in a voice that did not sound like his own.

His white face was contorted as he snarled like a wild animal.

"She is dedicated to Satan! She is his! Do not dare to disturb us, or I will kill her!"

He raised the knife.

As Charisa gave a murmur of horror, a Policeman who had appeared through the door at one side of the altar shot him in the arm.

Another Policeman coming in on the

other side of the Chapel shot him in the chest.

Gervais gave a screech of pain and fell backwards, the knife clattering to the floor.

There was a shriek of consternation from the men and women in the pews.

For the moment, they had been silenced by what had happened.

As they all began now to scream hysterically, Vincent rushed forward.

He picked Charisa up in his arms and wrapped the satin cover round her.

He carried her out through the side door from where the first Policeman had shot Gervais in the arm.

It all happened very swiftly.

Almost before she realised it, Vincent was carrying her along the passage and up the stairs.

The voices of the screaming Satanists gradually receded into the distance.

It was only as he reached her bed-room and carried her in that she burst into tears.

"It is all right, my precious. It is all over!" he said.

She was crying too tempestuously to hear him.

He lifted her onto the bed and covered her with the sheet and blankets.

Then he bent down to kiss the tears from

her eyes before stilling the trembling of her lips with his.

A surge of ecstasy swept through him like a ray of the sunlight.

When he raised his head he said:

"It is finished and it is entirely due to you, my darling, that I am a free man. How soon will you marry me?"

"Oh . . . Vincent . . . I love you," Charisa murmured. "But . . . supposing . . . they . . ."

"Leave everything to your father and the Chief Constable," Vincent said. "We have to be very grateful to them, for no one had any idea that the Policemen had slipped into the house, or that the Chapel was surrounded."

"And now . . . you are . . . really . . . safe?" Charisa asked.

He kissed her again before he said:

"You saved me, and now you have to look after me. We have a great deal to do together, so just forget what has happened, and think only of how busy we are going to be."

Charisa gave a little choked laugh.

"I do not . . . believe anyone has ever had such a . . . difficult time . . . in claiming his title and . . . estates!"

"The only thing I want to claim," Vincent answered, "is you. If you had not been here, anything might have happened. In fact, I am quite certain I would not have survived."

"But you have!" Charisa cried. "And, oh, darling, it is so wonderful to know that the Priory will be itself and Holy again."

Vincent smiled.

"Could it be anything else?" he asked. "I expect, if we knew the truth, throughout the ages there have been much worse things than French Satanists!"

Charisa looked up at him.

"You are . . . quite certain they have . . . not invoked . . . devils to . . . remain here and . . . frighten us?"

"If there are any devils left behind," Vincent said, "I am quite sure the spirits of the monks and of Saint Mawdelyn himself will deal with them!"

Charisa gave a little cry.

"That is the right answer! How could I have been so stupid as not to be aware that they would not let the Priory be hurt by Satan, if he really . . . does exist."

"All we are concerned with is our God, and we know He does exist!" Vincent said.

He kissed her again very gently before he said:

"And now, my darling, I must go downstairs to find out what is happening. Gervais is obviously badly injured. At the same time, he must leave the Priory and I am sure the Police will see to that."

"You . . . will come . . . back?" Charisa asked.

"You know I will," Vincent said. "Would you like to have Bessy with you?"

Charisa shook her head.

"Nobody but . . . you," she murmured.

He kissed her again.

Then, reluctantly, as he knew he must do his duty, he walked towards the door.

She thought as she watched him going out through the secret panel that he walked taller and his shoulders were squarer.

He looked exactly as the Marquis of Mawdelyn should look.

After he had gone she could not help crying again with happiness.

God had heard her prayers.

It was a week later that Charisa in her own bed-room at home was dressing for her wedding.

So much had happened that she could hardly believe it was actually her wedding-day.

It was wrong to wish anyone dead.

But it had in fact been a great relief when she learned that Gervais had died on his way to the Doctor.

His friends had been transported back to France.

But they had, however, been warned that if they ever set foot in England again, they would be arrested.

The Chaplain was wanted by the French Police for murder involving the sacrifice of a baby at a Satanist ceremony.

When *Madame* Dubus arrived in Paris, she learnt that her brother had died.

He was found in a public lavatory after injecting himself with an overdose of Morphine.

Vincent, as the new Marquis, had taken charge of the household and estate.

It was to the delight of all those who had served his uncle before him.

"Master Vincent," as many of the old servants could not help calling him, was returning everything to normal.

Charisa thought that Dawkins and Mrs. Bush both looked ten years younger.

Her father was only too willing to help Vincent in any way he could.

But she knew that as soon as they were married, her large fortune would be at his disposal.

They would then employ more people on the estate, while the household would return to the perfection it had known when she was a little girl.

Most important to Charisa, however, was that every day they spent together, Vincent's love for her grew.

It was clear that his desire to marry her had nothing to do with the fact that she was rich.

He loved her because she was a woman.

Also because, as he said himself, she was part of the Priory.

He could not imagine it as his home without her being there with him.

Now she looked in the mirror at her beautiful white wedding-gown which had come from London.

Her maid put the lace veil over her head and added her mother's diamond tiara.

As she did, Charisa thought all her dreams had come true.

"I shall be Vincent's wife," she told herself, "and we will be so happy at the Priory that we shall never want to go anywhere else."

She knew that London had no charm for her when she could be riding the horses they kept in the stables.

She loved moving through the great rooms.

She knew each one was sanctified by the monks who once again had fought against evil and won.

Gervais, to their relief, had not sold the jewelled Cross or the candlesticks from the Mawdelyn Chapel.

They were now back in their rightful place.

The Vicar had performed a very moving ceremony of exorcism to sweep away the last remnants of evil that might be lingering there.

The congregation had consisted only of Vincent, Charisa, and her father.

They made their responses to the prayers.

Then, as the Vicar blessed them with the jewelled Cross shining behind him, she felt that the monks were praising God.

She knew that all the household from her own home as well as the Priory would want to be present at their wedding.

The Service, therefore, was to be in the big Chapel.

To please her, the Vicar borrowed the jewelled Cross from the Abbot's Chapel for the ceremony.

"You will not be able to see it, my darling, for the flowers," Vincent told her. "The gardeners have been working round the clock to ensure that the Chapel is a worthy background for your beauty."

"All I want is that you should think I am . . . beautiful," Charisa answered.

"How could I think anything else?" he asked. "But it is not only your beautiful face that I love, it is your heart and soul."

He kissed her forehead and went on:

"Like a star you have guided and inspired me ever since I crept home, frightened that at any moment I would feel Gervais's knife between my shoulder blades."

Charisa put her arms round his neck.

"Do not frighten me, darling," she begged. "I can hardly believe there is not another wicked cousin trying to claim your title and estates!"

"There is one way for you to make certain there are not contenders of that kind," Vincent replied.

"How can I do that?" she asked.

"By giving me a son."

"Of course! Why did I not think of that?" Charisa asked.

She put her arms round his neck as she said very softly:

"The Priory should be filled with children. Remember how happy we were when we were young?"

Vincent did not answer.

He only kissed her passionately, demandingly, and she knew he was excited by what she had said.

Now, as she looked at herself in the

mirror, she hoped that he would always think her lovely.

Then he would never want to run after any other woman.

She had heard how in London many men were unfaithful to their wives, or wives to their husbands.

She had been shocked.

It had worried her that any man she married might, once they had grown used to her, look around for somebody new.

It was something her father had never done.

Now she felt sure that Vincent loved her as she loved him, not only with his heart, but with his soul.

A voice from the door asked:

"Are you ready, Miss Charisa? Th' carriage is at th' door and th' Colonel's waiting in th' hall."

"I am coming!" Charisa replied.

She took one last look in the mirror.

"Please, God," she prayed, "make him always think that I am as lovely as I look to-day."

Then she turned and walked down the stairs to where her father was waiting for her.

The carriage was drawn by a new team of perfectly matched black horses.

The Colonel had given them to Vincent as a wedding-present.

"I was at Tattersall's," he explained, "and I could not resist them. I was going to buy them for myself, but then I thought how beautiful Charisa would look sitting behind them, and so, my boy, they are yours!"

"I cannot begin to thank you," Vincent had said, "though all that really matters is that you are giving me Charisa!"

The Colonel had laughed.

"I think, if the truth were known, my permission was never asked one way or the other! But suffice to say that I would rather have you as my son-in-law than any other man in the world!"

Inside the carriage Charisa slipped her hand into her father's.

"I am so excited that you and Vincent are going to build a race-course together," she said. "It means that I will be able to see you every day, and I could not lose you, Papa!"

"I have no intention of losing you," the Colonel replied. "I have a great many plans for both our Estates, which I think now must eventually be joined together."

"Oh, Papa, what a wonderful idea!" Charisa exclaimed. "And I know it will please and thrill Vincent."

"You can leave me to look after things

while you are on your honeymoon," the Colonel said. "I know Vincent will be thinking of nothing but you, and you will be thinking of him."

"You are quite right," Charisa said, "but if you buy us any more horses, we shall be forced to enlarge the stables!"

"I have thought of that already!" the Colonel remarked.

They both laughed.

As they came in sight of the Priory, Charisa felt her heart beating excitedly.

Dawkins was waiting at the top of the steps to welcome her.

The footmen in the hall had never looked smarter.

The Chapel was filled to capacity with the households from both houses.

The people on the estate were there too, including all the Farmers and their wives.

As Charisa walked up the aisle she felt they were all part of one great family, a family which had started when the monks built the Priory.

The first Abbot had brought it the blessing of the Saint after whom he had been named.

His own blessing had remained all down the centuries.

Charisa and Vincent knelt for the final

blessing on their marriage.

As they did so, she thought that no one could be more blessed than they were, and no one could be happier.

Then it was all over and she was waiting in the Master Bed-room.

Because Gervais had slept there, this room also had been exorcised.

Now it was fragrant with the scent of lilies and other flowers.

They had been arranged by the gardeners.

The fireplace was filled with them, and there were huge vases on either side of the bed.

Vincent came into the room and stood for a moment just looking at his wife.

He was thinking that nothing could be more lovely, and she looked like a flower herself.

Charisa held out her arms, but for a moment he did not move.

"Can I really own anything so precious?" he asked.

"I am yours . . . all yours, my darling," she whispered.

Slowly he went towards her.

Then he sat down on the bed, just as he had when he had come through the secret panel.

"I feel as if I am in a dream," he said, "and

I am only afraid I may wake up."

"You are . . . awake," Charisa answered softly, "and I am here with . . . you."

"My star, who has guided and saved me," Vincent said. "There is so much I want to say to you, but I cannot put it into words."

"There is . . . no need . . . for words," Charisa murmured. "My heart is . . . calling to your . . . heart and I love you . . . Vincent!"

He moved in beside her and took her into his arms.

"I love, adore, and worship you!" he said. "But that does not adequately express what I am feeling at this moment."

Then he was kissing her, kissing her passionately, demandingly, fiercely, as if he were afraid that after all, he might lose her.

To Charisa it was as if the world itself swung dizzily around them.

She too was moving in the dream.

It was a dream of love, so perfect that it was impossible to describe it.

They were no longer human — no longer on earth.

She was the star that Vincent thought her to be, and he was glittering with her.

A light emanated from them both, joining them and making them a part of the Divine.

"I love you . . . I love you . . . !"

The words were being spoken with their hearts — their souls.

It was love which swept through them, making it impossible to think, only to feel.

She belonged to Vincent.

They had faced fear and darkness and fought Satan to find each other.

The evil had been swept away.

They knew that the holiness of the Priory would in the future sweep away anything that tried to hurt them.

"I love you . . . I love you . . . !"

It was the song of angels, the chanting of the monks.

She could hear it vibrating on the air, hear it in the beating of their hearts, in the ecstasy that Vincent's kisses evoked in them both.

They were no longer two people, but one for all time.

The blessing of God was theirs.

It would pass to their children, their children's children, and all those who came after them.

It was the blessing of Love which is Divine.

About the Author

Barbara Cartland, the world's most famous romantic novelist, who is also an historian, playwright, lecturer, political speaker and television personality, has now written over 552 books and sold over six hundred and fifty million copies all over the world.

She has also had many historical works published and has written four autobiographies as well as the biographies of her mother and that of her brother, Ronald Cartland, who was the first Member of Parliament to be killed in the last war. This book has a preface by Sir Winston Churchill and has been republished with an introduction by Sir Arthur Bryant.

Love at the Helm, a novel written with the help and inspiration of the late Earl Mountbatten of Burma, Great Uncle of His Royal Highness The Prince of Wales, is being sold for the Mountbatten Memorial Trust.

She has broken the world record for the last sixteen years by writing an average of twenty-three books a year. In the *Guinness Book of Records* she is listed as the world's top-selling author.

Miss Cartland in 1978 sang an Album of Love Songs with the Royal Philharmonic Orchestra.

In private life Barbara Cartland, who is a Dame of the Order of St. John of Jerusalem, Chairman of the St. John Council in Hertfordshire and Deputy President of the St. John Ambulance Brigade, has fought for better conditions and salaries for Midwives and Nurses.

She championed the cause for the Elderly in 1956 invoking a Government Enquiry into the "Housing Condition of Old People."

In 1962 she had the Law of England changed so that Local Authorities had to provide camps for their own Gypsies. This has meant that since then thousands and thousands of Gypsy children have been able to go to School, which they had never been able to do in the past, as their caravans were moved every twenty-four hours by the Police.

There are now fourteen camps in Hertfordshire and Barbara Cartland has her own Romany Gypsy Camp called Barbaraville by the Gypsies.

Her designs "Decorating with Love" are being sold all over the U.S.A. and the National Home Fashions League made her, in 1981, "Woman of Achievement."

She is unique in that she was one and two in the Dalton list of Best Sellers, and one week had four books in the top twenty.

Barbara Cartland's book *Getting Older, Growing Younger* has been published in Great Britain and the U.S.A. and her fifth cookery book, *The Romance of Food*, is now being used by the House of Commons.

In 1984 she received at Kennedy Airport America's Bishop Wright Air Industry Award for her contribution to the development of aviation. In 1931 she and two R.A.F. Officers thought of, and carried, the first aeroplane-towed glider airmail.

During the War she was Chief Lady Welfare Officer in Bedfordshire, looking after 20,000 Servicemen and women. She thought of having a pool of Wedding Dresses at the War Office so a Service Bride could hire a gown for the day.

She bought 1,000 gowns without coupons for the A.T.S., the W.A.A.F.'s and the W.R.E.N.S. In 1945 Barbara Cartland received the Certificate of Merit from Eastern Command.

In 1964 Barbara Cartland founded the National Association for Health of which she is the President, as a front for all the

Health Stores and for any product made as alternative medicine.

This is now a £65 million turnover a year, with one-third going in export.

In January 1988 she received *La Médaille de Vermeil de la Ville de Paris*. This is the highest award to be given in France by the City of Paris. She has sold 25 million books in France.

In March 1988 Barbara Cartland was asked by the Indian Government to open their Health Resort outside Delhi. This is almost the largest Health Resort in the world.

Barbara Cartland was received with great enthusiasm by her fans, who feted her at a reception in the City, and she received the gift of an embossed plate from the Government.

Barbara Cartland was made a Dame of the Order of the British Empire in the 1991 New Year's Honours List by Her Majesty The Queen for her contribution to Literature and also for her years of work for the community.

The employees of Thorndike Press hope you have enjoyed this Large Print book. All our Thorndike and Wheeler Large Print titles are designed for easy reading, and all our books are made to last. Other Thorndike Press Large Print books are available at your library, through selected bookstores, or directly from us.

For information about titles, please call:

(800) 223-1244

or visit our Web site at:

www.gale.com/thorndike
www.gale.com/wheeler

To share your comments, please write:

Publisher
Thorndike Press
295 Kennedy Memorial Drive
Waterville, ME   04901

DATE DUE

Bye FEB 2 8 2003; Lyndorski	bnks	
MAR 3 0	OC 26 '04	
	Custeau	
SEP 2 4 2003 Bye	Trxvers	
OCT 3 1 2003 Hathaway MAR 2 5 2004 O'Leary	JAN – 3 2009	2009
JUN – 1 2000		
June 22nd		
MCD		
JUN 2 3 2004		
CYWD JUL 0 7 2004		
MCD		
JUN 2 7 2004		